First Loves Lost

by Hank Lajoie

Order this book online at www.trafford.com
or email orders@trafford.com

Most Trafford titles are also available at major online book retailers.

Note for Librarians: A cataloguing record for this book is available from Library and Archives Canada at www.collectionscanada.ca/amicus/index-e.html

Printed in Victoria, BC, Canada.

ISBN: 978-1-4269-0535-3 (sc)
ISBN: 978-1-4269-0536-0 (eBook)

Our mission is to efficiently provide the world's finest, most comprehensive book publishing service, enabling every author to experience success. To find out how to publish your book, your way, and have it available worldwide, visit us online at www.trafford.com

Trafford rev. 08/26/09

Trafford PUBLISHING® www.trafford.com

North America & international
toll-free: 1 888 232 4444 (USA & Canada)
phone: 250 383 6864 ♦ fax: 812 355 4082

Foreword

Most of us have experienced the loss of our first loves. In most cases, we simply outgrew the relationships and our "firsts" had little impact on the rest of our lives. In this story of lost loves, however, the losses for four of the characters raise the question *What if?* Adolescents have to deal with sexual discovery and loss; painful maturing; traumatic events; and a roller coaster ride between the emotions of happiness and sadness.

In an attempt to recreate their first love, Larry and Ashley, brought back together after a misunderstanding, find the adolescent magic is gone. Ashley goes her own way and never marries.

Larry and his wife Penny have an adopted Korean son and he and his stepsister bring new meaning to the term *sibling love.*

All characters are fictitious (except for the pig), the events are products of imagination, and any similarity with actual events (except for the pig) is pure coincidence.

I owe a debt of gratitude to my team of proofreaders: Lyn Tierney, Julie Wessling and my wife Pat. They found more errors than any author should be entitled to make.

Chapter 1

Laurent St. Jacques was a rather classy sounding name for a kid who grew up during the years of World War II . . . you know, the one that was to end all wars . . . or was that World War I? In any event, he grew up in the small town of Peabody, Massachusetts. He lived on Tremont Street for most of his younger years, but at age 11, he moved to Northend Street, not far away. It was a quiet, almost sleepy residential street. Most of the houses were two-story, two-family dwellings, nestled snugly between the states of *well maintained* and *disrepair.*

It was only three blocks from the nearest bus stop and he could go almost anywhere in his small world for a dime. He usually walked to downtown Peabody, but rode the bus to go to the Salem Willows, a beach and amusement park. More often than not, he found it more expedient to hitch a ride, saving his dimes for other pleasures at The Willows.

Northend Street was a Norman Rockwell neighborhood, both in appearance and in the social mores of the time. The characters were no different. The worn out shoes, sloppy sox and rumpled clothing were things they considered badges of honor for their status; poor but proud and clean, most of the time.

Every back yard boasted a Victory Garden and neighborhood children enjoyed a significant number of raw vegetables there for the picking. The occasional raw carrot, fresh tomato or fresh green beans were not only supplements to their diet, but they often satisfied genuine pangs of hunger. Some of the families kept chickens and rabbits. One of his neighbors, Mr. Silva kept a pig in his back yard, where he had built a shed and sty for him (or her; Laurent never really knew).

Just a block away, an elementary school provided plenty of room for play; including a real baseball field with a backstop. There was also ample space for football in the fall and no one every worried about liability insurance, nor did they try to limit the use of the schoolyard and its facilities.

It was there that he met Ashley Cummings, a bratty little girl who was as crude as any boy ever was. When the boys got together to play war games or cowboys and Indians, Ashley inserted herself into the group. She asserted herself as the leader, no less, taking control at the first opportunity. Fortunately, as the games progressed, they tended to forget that Ashley was a girl and she proved to be a worthy adversary in whatever game was underway.

To say that at age twelve Ashley was a tomboy doesn't tell much of her story. She was at best, unattractive and brash. One would think that there was some sort of bias toward her, or at least some of the boys did back then. They were all in that pre-teen era of their lives when interest in the sexes had yet to materialize fully.

Ashley was as gangly as girls get. She had skinny little girl legs, with knees that were already adult-sized. She had elbows so sharp she probably could have punctured a coconut with them to get at its milk. She wore her red-orange hair short. Not so wise for someone who had ears like . . . well, some of the boys called her "Dumbo-ears."

She had a mouthful of crooked, jagged teeth that she seemed to delight in flashing in broad smiles to the many antagonists she somehow managed to accumulate in her entourage. If the old wives' tale is true that freckles are where angels kissed her when she was a baby, this girl had a vast fan club of angels.

Everyone knows that boys at that age love to spit and many were to become downright proficient. However, there weren't many boys who could challenge Ashley to a spitting contest and win. They would draw a circle in the dirt and back off five paces, and then attempt to spit that distance and land their juicy projectiles within the circle. Ashley usually won. She knew how high to arch her accumulated spit and how wide to spit to compensate for the wind. Ashley came up with a bit more interesting approach to these contests by drawing straws to see who would stand within the circle. It was a certainty that one of the boys had to clean off his shoes before Ashley was through.

At that age, the wide range of foul words one could learn had fascinated many of them. Ashley again proved to be the one to excel. Not only was her vocabulary impressive, she actually knew where and when to apply each cuss-word in a grammatically correct manner. She also possessed a wisdom beyond her years, using her choice vocabulary only when certain that no adults were nearby to hear.

The neighborhood boys, plus Ashley, became a loyal band of friends that stayed together through their early teens.

Chapter 2

The afternoon matinee was Errol Flynn's *They Died With Their Boots On*, a half-accurate account of *Custer's Last Stand*. While most of the boys were praising the brave heroics of the soldiers under Custer's command, Ashley insisted that the true heroes were the Indians. She said that they were braver, smarter and more worthy of praise and honor. Of course, the boys saw this as some sort of treason. Ashley asserted that Custer was stupid to engage so many hostile Indians.

Bobby Carson observed that if they were to restage the battle, Custer would surely win.

"Are you nuts?" Ashley challenged.

Bobby shouted back, "It was just a movie! Ain't no way some Indians could beat Errol Flynn; Custer, I mean."

"Oh, yeah? Well, you guys be the soldiers and Laurent and I will be the Indians. Betcha the battle ends just the same."

"We can't do that battle," said Joey Martin. "We need bows and arrows and guns . . . too much stuff."

"Not really," Ashley said. "Everyone get a towel and get it soakin' wet. When you get hit with a wet towel, you're dead and out of the game."

"There are four of us and only two of you," Bobby observed. "How's that gonna work?"

"Everybody gets one towel; me and Laurent get two towels. That way me and Laurent have enough to wipe out all four of you. We'll win, 'cause Indians are smarter."

Joey interjected, "Custer was outnumbered, but you Indians are now."

"And when we wipe you guys out, it will just prove that the Indians were better, like I said," Ashley replied with a pert little smile.

They scattered to their individual homes to pick up towels. Getting the towels soaking wet was easy; carrying them through the house without dripping all over the place was the hard part. When they reassembled, most of the boys had water signs down pants legs and on shoes. Ashley arrived with a small bucket filled with water, her two towels immersed therein. Laurent immersed his two towels with hers.

"OK," Ashley began, "here are the rules. You guys are the soldiers. Bobby, you can be Custer. Laurent and me will be the Indians. You guys stand here and me and him will charge from the porch over there. When you're hit with a towel, you fall down and stay down. You're dead!"

"This is stupid," Joey said. "But it sounds like fun anyway. You two are gonna get wet!"

"We'll see," Ashley said. "C'mon, Laurent. We have to plan our attack."

Ashley and Laurent went to the porch and Ashley laid out her battle plan. Each of them would take one soaking wet towel and rush at the group. Ashley would break to the left; Laurent would rush to the right. They would toss their soggy missiles and rush back to the porch, re-arm and rush again, just like the Indians did in the movie. It sounded simple.

They fished out one towel each and with Ashley shrieking like an Indian, set upon the four "soldiers." Before they got to within throwing range, Laurent also started whooping a war cry and cocked his arm to unleash the first towel. Just as he released it, a sopping, wet towel hit him right in the face. Fortunately, his watery missile also found a target, hitting Joey flush in the stomach. The towel released enough water so that it looked like Joey had wet his pants. Before Laurent could start laughing at that sight, another towel caught him squarely in the chest. As he lowered himself to the ground as required by Ashley's rules, he saw her unleash a towel, catching Tony Silva squarely in the back of his head. As Ashley ran back to the porch unscathed, her second towel still in reserve, Bobby and Stanley Mason were standing, holding their "ammunition."

A sinister smile crossed Bobby's face and Laurent thought at the time that he had never seen such an evil leer directed at Ashley. Without a word, he was challenging her to accept her fate . . . death at the hands of General George Custer. Of course, Ashley would accept the challenge.

With a blood-curdling scream, she scooped up a towel in each hand and charged the two boys. A wet towel fell at her feet as she stopped short to avoid being hit. Stanley, now unarmed, couldn't avoid Ashley's accurate throw. Her towel hit him in the face with such force that he lost his balance and fell.

"Oh, shit, General Custer. I been hit!" Stanley shouted.

Bobby hesitated in response to Stanley's call and it was just enough for Ashley to close quickly and throw her last sopping wet towel. Bobby prepared to whirl and throw his towel, when Ashley's towel struck him on the side of his face. He never launched his own towel.

With water running and dripping down inside his shirt, Bobby glared at Ashley and shouted, "You cheated!"

"Like hell, I did!" she shouted back. "I told you the Indians were smarter, didn't I?"

Bobby approached and stood toe to toe with Ashley. "If you was no damned girl, I'd pop you one right in the nose!"

Ashley placed her hands on his chest and pushed him away. He stepped back up to her and did the same. The others gasped as his hands came in contact with her chest. Although no better endowed than most girls at twelve, there was the hint of a "chest" and they all knew that boys didn't touch girls there (although they were not yet sure why).

Ashley's right hand seemed to shoot forward at the speed of light and met Bobby's nose. It was not a little girl's slap, either. The fist, balled up tight, served up as good a right cross as the champion, Joe Louis might have delivered. Bobby's head rocked backward and it seemed that the blood began to flow almost instantly. It was at this very moment that the supreme disaster occurred. Ashley's mother saw what had happened and was rushing toward the group! The boys were all slightly confused. Do they run away? Do they just point at Ashley and let things happen as they may? The thought of sacrificing Ashley to the wrath of her parent was not an acceptable choice. Before anyone could rise to her defense however, her mother bellowed at Bobby, "How dare you touch my daughter there?"

Bobby stood still, blood streaming from his nose, his mind a total blank. He could think of nothing to say in his own defense.

"Get that nose checked, you naughty little boy!" Ashley's mom said.

Ashley smiled as her mother led her away; then they suddenly stopped.

Bellowed is the only word to describe the outburst from Ashley's mom that followed.

"Are those my best guest towels?" She picked up two soggy rags, which were indeed, her best guest towels.

Ashley caught all kinds of hell, but maintained her leadership role in the group. The boys had a deep, abiding respect for this ungainly tomboy who could out-cuss all of them and who, somehow, *earned* that respect . . . a respect normally reserved for members of their own sex. Without the necessary physical attributes, Ashley was truly "one of the guys."

It was nearly a week before they were all together again, which was Bobby's first chance to apologize to Ashley for touching her "there."

"Hey," she responded. "You pushed me and I thought you wanted to fight."

"I don't fight with no girls," Bobby responded.

"Well don't worry about it; ain't nothin' there but my flat old chest."

"Yeah, but boys shouldn't do that."

"What, this?" she asked as she grabbed both his wrists and placed his hands on her chest. Bobby looked horrified and pulled his hands away. Then Ashley surprised them further as she took her hands and rubbed Bobby's chest.

"Hey! Stop that," Bobby said.

"Ain't no difference. Just chests. Nothin' different." She turned to Laurent and winked, adding, "Yet." She smiled at Bobby's obvious discomfort as he blushed.

"You guys want a feel, too?" Ashley asked.

To this day, they could not remember if they wanted to. There was a mystery of sorts here, but they all said "no" in unison.

"Good. So forget about it."

They sat on the porch steps and made small talk, but Ashley couldn't help but revive the "mystery."

"There's really nothin' to feel here now, anyway," she said as her hands fondled that area where some day breasts would appear. "But someday, I'll have tits just like all the older girls. Then you better not even *think* about touchin' 'em."

"Don't have to worry about me," Bobby said as he mocked protecting his nose.

"I felt tits before," Tony said. "They was real soft."

"What?" Ashley looked at Tony putting on her best glare. They were all suddenly interested.

"Wow," Bobby said in awe. "What happened?"

"My big sister and me was playin' around and she started ticklin' me. I reached up to tickle her, but because I was tickled, I grabbed her right there."

"Wow," Bobby repeated.

"Bet she belted you one," Joey chimed in.

"Naw. She just smiled at me and got up and that was it."

"Wow."

Ashley was grinning, her snaggly teeth gleaming as the sun bounced off them.

Tony continued, "I was scared at first when I saw where my hands were, but we were just playin' around and it was an accident. My sister thought so, too."

"Wow," Bobby said, seemingly at a loss for words.

"Will you cut out that 'wow' stuff? You sound like a broke record," Stanley said.

"What's all the fuss? It doesn't sound like it's a big deal," Joey said. "Why would a guy want to touch them, anyway?"

Ashley smiled again, saying, "It's supposed to make a girl horny, I've heard."

"Horny?" Laurent asked. Although he had heard the word, he still wasn't sure what it meant.

"Yeah. Makes 'em hot," Stanley said. "My brother told me that girls like to play a lot before they do anythin'."

"Do anything? Like what?" Bobby asked.

"Like kissin', you jerk," Ashley said with a giggle.

"Oh," Bobby said.

With that, their knowledge of such things was exhausted and the subject quickly turned to Red Sox baseball and the likelihood that they may win the pennant this year.

Chapter 3

In those days, creativity was the name of the game . . . any game. When they didn't have enough equipment to play baseball or football they improvised, creating games based on a current movie. They couldn't remember the movie title, but it involved a manhunt, so they decided one day to create a new game. They rounded up all the returnable tonic (soft drink) bottles they could find and turned them in for a five-cent deposit return. Enough people just threw the bottles out in the trash that they always managed to scrape up bus fare or movie money (matinees cost a dime, popcorn a nickel).

Their manhunt game allowed each player to have two dimes for bus fare. One was to go somewhere in town (anywhere) and another to return home. Players left separately after drawing straws to see who would be the "it" called *The Blacksmith.* The straws were all the same except for the blacksmith's straw that had a special mark on it. No one knew who the blacksmith was, except the one who drew the tainted straw.

They went their separate ways, each getting off the bus at a different stop. Then they just walked around, hoping that if they met one of the group, he or she wasn't the blacksmith. When they did meet a member of the group, they were supposed to stop and talk to them. The conversations always started with, "Are you the blacksmith?" If so, he inherited the straw. He then had to go on the hunt for another member of the group to pass it on.

The game had a strict three-hour time limit with the only prize being the pride of eluding *The Blacksmith.*

Ashley was the best blacksmith ever. She had an uncanny sense for figuring out where the boys would go. The boys just wandered and usually went to their favorite places. Ashley would always be there and when she was the blacksmith, she avoided that first question and played along. Then, when you least expected it, she would hand over the marked straw. Wearing a big grin, she would say, "Have fun findin' a new blacksmith, you jerk."

On one of these outings, Ashley was the first one Laurent met in the downtown area. Neither was the blacksmith, so they walked together for a while. They were approaching the local theatre when Ashley spotted Bobby about a block away.

"Quick," she said as she grabbed Laurent by the wrist and pulled him into the theatre's entryway. "I think Bobby's the blacksmith."

"But the rules say we have to greet him and ask the question."

"Look, the usher's not there. The movie must be half over. C'mon!"

With that, she pulled him along toward the entrance and they were quickly inside and out of sight. They sat well back so no one would see them come in and sit down.

"You're gonna get us in trouble," Laurent whispered.

"Shhh! Just watch the movie."

"But . . ."

She put her hands on his head and pulled him toward her and she kissed him! "Now just be quiet or I'll do it again."

"We can't" . . . and she *did* do it again!

This time Laurent just sat back. He looked at the screen and two guys were fighting over something or other. He turned and looked at Ashley. She stared straight ahead, and then turned toward him.

"Nice, huh?" she said with a smile. Then she moved closer, took his arm, and placed it around her shoulders.

Laurent honestly couldn't understand the feelings that coursed through his body at that time because he had not yet learned the words and meanings to express them. He pulled her toward him until the armrest between the seats pressed against his rib cage. Soon it started to hurt, but he didn't want to let go of her. He remembered thinking, *Wow!*

She rested her head against his and soon they exchanged a few more kisses. At that age, their kisses were innocent little pecks, with lips pressed tightly together.

That's all that happened. They didn't even hold hands walking back to a bus stop to go home. They had exceeded the three-hour time limit so were disqualified. That was supposed to be a fate worse than being caught in the role of *The Blacksmith* at game's end. To Laurent, it was a small price to pay for a couple of hours of such pleasure.

The next day, Ashley and Laurent sat on her front porch.

"About yesterday," he began.

"Fun, wasn't it?"

"Yeah, but . . ."

"Did you notice that in the movie when they were kissin' they had their mouths opened a little? We didn't do that."

He looked at her and saw that she wore a half-smile as she looked at him.

"I didn't notice," he said. "I just liked it."

"Look," she said as she parted her lips slightly. "Just like this. Do it."

He parted his lips slightly as she had done. "Like this?"

"Like that," she said, and then kissed him. "Just like that."

They looked at each other, saying nothing.

Suddenly, she got to her feet and said, "Let's go."

She stepped off the porch and started walking down the street. He followed along. They walked side by side for a while until Ashley broke the silence.

"You know, your name's a pain in the ass to say. Why don't you use a nickname, like Larry? Americans named Lawrence do it and Laurent is French for the same thing, isn't it?"

"I suppose. You can call me Larry if you want."

"Yup. I want."

With that, she slipped her hand into his and they walked together quietly toward the schoolyard just a block away. Larry's first thought was what the other guys might think if they were seen holding hands, but the warmth of her hand in his quickly dispelled any thought that the guys might think anything that mattered.

When they got to the school building, they walked around to the back where they were out of sight. Larry didn't know why they had come here, but there were all sorts of strange sensations assaulting his body. He felt flushed; his heart was somehow beating against his eardrums. He felt generally ill at ease, but it was enjoyable, too. Then Ashley just stopped, turned to him and planted a kiss on him. Their arms were suddenly around each other and their young bodies pressed together. As he was enjoying the kiss and the pressure of their bodies against each other, Ashley astounded him again! He suddenly felt her tongue gently probing his lips. He was tempted to pull away . . . it was disgusting! But, just for a moment. Soon, his tongue also brushed softly against her lips.

Something went off inside his head. It wasn't a bell or any percussive alarm. It was an awareness that anything this wonderful between a boy and a girl *had* to be a sin! He wanted more, but more of what? Kissing was wonderful, but was that all there was to it?

"We have to do this more often," Ashley said as she pushed herself away.

He was stunned and speechless. How could she just back off like that? He didn't want to offend her, so he just shrugged and said, "I guess."

"Didn't you like it?"

"Sure I did, but I never kissed a girl like that before." With that, he grabbed her and pulled her to him, planting a kiss firmly on her mouth, probing with his tongue and pressing himself into her. She resisted only slightly and when he buried his face in her neck, she just giggled.

"Enough, Larry. I'm getting uncomfortable."

"Me, too," he said. "I'm feelin' kinda funny."

Ashley smiled at him and looked into his eyes. "There has to be somethin' beyond the kissin', don't you think?"

"Don't know, but I hope so."

They kissed again and Larry had no idea what prompted him to do what he did next. His arms were around her and he suddenly realized that his hands had moved down and had firmly pressed onto her buttocks. He pulled her tightly against his lower body. His own body responded with a reaction that he had only experienced at times when he was asleep. He awoke with a condition that he had been told was perfectly natural and nothing to worry about. Now, here was that reaction and he was wide awake, kissing a girl he considered to be *one of the guys*. What on earth could *this* mean?

Ashley quickly removed his hands and backed away. "What the hell are you doing?" she asked.

He stammered something, including the words, "I don't know."

"Well, don't do it again." A pause; "I liked it, but don't do it again."

"I liked it, too."

"I think we need to find out what's happenin' to us," she said.

"Yeah. I don't think it's bad, though, do you?"

Ashley looked thoughtful. "The question is if it feels good and you like it, is that OK?"

"Huh?'

"You know," she went on, "what if what we're doin' is a sin? Would it still feel good? I remember Father Kelly sayin' that most sins feel good while you're sinnin'."

"But if it's a sin, we can just confess it and we're forgiven, right?"

Ashley looked at him, grinned and kissed him. This time, *her* hands wandered. He was immobilized!

She pushed away and took his hand, leading him back home and he responded like a docile puppy.

"What a wondrous and glorious creature was this Ashley of mine," he thought. "Dare I call her *mine?"*

Chapter 4

The neighborhood kids never really understood why Mr. Silva kept a pig penned up in his back yard. Chickens and rabbits had their own distinctive odors, but the pig was another thing. They wallowed around in mud and their own wastes and smelled to high heaven. When the wind blew, the disgusting odor wafted throughout the neighborhood and seemed to permeate everything.

Mr. Silva and many of his neighbors were Portuguese and Mr. Silva had a small grocery store on the corner about a block away. Shopping there, local families were introduced to a Portuguese sausage called *linguisa,* of which some were quite fond. It was spicy, juicy with a wide range of fatty substances and had a wonderful flavor. The mystery behind its makeup was about to be resolved. It was time for Mr. Silva's unfortunate porcine family member to repay the many kindnesses the Silva family had provided. None of the guys knew if the pig had a name. Hopefully not. They just couldn't understand how anyone could slaughter a member of the family that could be called by name.

Tony Silva was genuinely excited. "We're gonna slaughter the pig!" he shouted.

"Why?" Ashley asked. "Is somethin' wrong with it?"

"Naw," Tony said. "We're just gonna eat it."

"Eat it?" Larry was incredulous. "You eat the pig?"

"Sure," Bobby said. "Even I know that's where pork chops come from."

Maybe it was the realization that Bobby was, in fact, right, but it was a long time before Larry could enjoy a pork chop again. Fortunately, his family couldn't afford them that often and his mom's cooking prowess dictated using most of their meat ration coupons on hamburger or chuck roast (he didn't know for sure *where* they came from).

"Listen," Tony said. "My daddy said we could help."

"We?" Ashley asked. "You mean all us kids?"

"Sure," Tony said. "When the pig is dead they burn all the hair off it and the skin gets all black from the flame. Then it has to be scrubbed clean before they cut it all up."

"No thanks," Larry said.

"That's sickenin'!" Joey Martin chimed in.

"Why not?" Of course, it was Ashley. "How many times are we gonna get to see that? Let's all do it."

"You must be sick in the head," Stanley said to Ashley.

"What a bunch of sissies," Ashley teased. "I bet Larry will do it, too, huh Larry?"

"Sure." He shrugged. He couldn't let Ashley down and he sure didn't want her to think he was a sissy. He quickly added, "And what kind of a sissy would a guy be if he couldn't help out a girl with a job like that?"

Tony and Ashley were beaming. The others just glared at Larry. The gauntlet had been thrown at their collective feet and not wanting to be called sissies, they capitulated.

"Saturday mornin' about eight, they're gonna kill it. We have to be there by eight-thirty to get started, OK?" Tony said.

Saturday was two days away and it was obvious that they were nervous about this strange undertaking that none of them had ever experienced. When they talked about it, they spoke in hushed tones as if someone might overhear and think they were some kind of ghouls.

Saturday morning, about seven-thirty, Ashley knocked on Larry's door. His mother answered the knock and turned to him.

"It's that scrawny Cummings kid for you," she said. "What kind of trouble are you two up to?"

"Nothin' much," Ashley interjected. "Just gonna help kill a pig."

His mother's eyebrows arched violently, eyes popping wide. "What?"

"Mr. Silva is gonna kill his pig, mom," Larry said. "We're just gonna help with little kids jobs. We ain't gonna kill it. Mr. Silva is."

His mother looked at them with a vacant expression. She fished a cigarette out of a rumpled pack, lit it and blew out some smoke. "Don't get all dirty and smelly," she said.

With that, Ashley and Larry were quickly out the door.

"C'mon," she said. "Let's get right over to Mr. Silva's."

"But we don't have to be there until eight-thirty."

"I know, but I want to see how they kill it."

They were walking briskly toward the Silva house. The expression on Ashley's face was one of eager anticipation. Larry wondered about her fascination with how something was about to be killed. When they arrived they stayed out of the way, and the men and women of the neighborhood prepared for the ritual that would end the poor pig's life.

The men, wearing rubber boots, aprons and gloves entered the pigsty. The pig seemed to know that something was afoot and, sensing danger, began to squeal as it darted back and forth, trying to avoid capture. Larry had seen the pig a number of times but never realized how huge he (or she) was. When finally cornered and the men fell upon it, the pig's cries became deafening. The legs were quickly tied and the hind legs were roped into a block and tackle. The pig was hoisted in the air and one of the men deftly slit the throat. The cut was deep and blood gushed from the opening the knife had made and collected in a bucket. Tony told Larry and Ashley that they would make something called blood sausage from it, but they doubted that.

They put the pig on a table made of rough boards and sawhorses. They burned off the hair and the kids soaped it down and used pumice stones to clean the skin thoroughly. None of them was talking much, afraid that talking would require more breathing than necessary resulting in a need to vomit. By the time the men opened it up and removed its innards, Bobby, Joey and Stanley had already gone home to clean up. Ashley stood with Larry, squeezing his hand and watching intently. Her first sign of revulsion came when they removed the pig's intestines and emptied them of their contents. She watched, muttered "yuk" a time or two, but said little else.

The women were now gathering all sorts of meat scraps, a glob of fat here and there and anything else the men deemed appropriate to toss into a large bowl. From those ingredients, the women pounded, ground and mixed by hand the concoction that made up that wondrous, delicious sausage called *linguisa*.

The next step in the process was the one that put *linguisa* into the same temporary category of, as Ashley put it, "yuk."

The pig's intestines now cleared of their waste product and rinsed clean with wine, were stuffed with the ingredients previously prepared. Once filled, the women pinched the intestine about every foot and twisted it tightly, thus forming sausages. He had never thought to ask what held hot dogs and sausages together, but to this day, whenever Larry bit into a tough-skinned sausage, the morning of the pig slaughter came to mind.

"How'd you like that?" Ashley asked Larry as they walked home.

"I don't think I want to do it again."

"Me, neither," Ashley said excitedly, "but wasn't it great just getting to see somethin' like that? We may never see anythin' like that again."

"That suits me," he said. "The way that poor pig squealed made me feel sorry for it."

"Oh, it was just scared. Tony told me that it doesn't hurt the pig. Didn't you notice how it stopped squealin' as soon as they cut its throat?"

"Gosh, Ashley," he said, "it couldn't squeal even if it wanted to after they cut it like that. And all that blood!"

"Listen, Larry, every time you eat meat, you're eatin' something that had to be killed. You seen how we kill chickens, ain't you? And fish? My dad used to gut them while they were still alive when we went fishin'."

"Let's talk about somethin' else."

"OK. Do you think it's true that Chinamen eat cats?"

"Oh, for Pete's sake, Ashley. What's got into you?"

"Damn. You sound like my mother. *What's got into you?*" She mocked.

"We just watched somethin' get killed! Ain't that botherin' you?"

"Why should it? I didn't kill it and it's gonna be ate up, so its dyin' was good."

"Well, I don't think I could eat any of it after being part of its death. I mean I had my hands on it. I cleaned it. I heard it die."

"Boy, you're pretty sensitive about that, huh? Real feelings. I like that in my man."

She said my man! "Just what is that supposed to mean?"

"You know," she said. "We do things together; we go places together. That's what boy friends and girl friends do. Aren't we like that?"

"Sure," he responded quickly. *Boy friend and girl friend . . . Wow!*

They joined their smelly hands and began to wonder what their folks would say when they got a whiff of their clothes. They hadn't had to come in contact with anything to smell the way they did. The odors were so thick and heavy, they permeated their clothing and indisputably put them at the scene of the crime. Larry realized that he was focusing on their smells rather than pursue the boy friend-girl friend subject any further, for fear it would result in being less than he hoped it would be.

"Besides," she said, "we're twelve now and it's probably about time I had a boy friend and you had a girl friend. Steady."

"Steady?"

"Yeah, you know. You don't go with another girl and I don't go with another boy. Steady."

"Sure."

It was then he wondered how he and Ashley had become so close. For one thing, there were other girls in the neighborhood a lot prettier than Ashley and they acted like girls rather than as one of the guys. He was definitely attracted to her and when they kissed, everything about it seemed right. Of course, at that age, he couldn't find the words to express all that he felt, but he was old enough to know that it was good. He was convinced that he was in love and hoped that Ashley felt the same way. That was something to explore in the near future.

The day was not over. During supper, there was a knock on the door and Tony delivered a small thank you from his dad; three foot-long lengths of *linguisa.* Larry's mom put it into the icebox, Tony left and they finished supper.

Later, sitting with Ashley on the front porch, they had a brief discussion on the merits of *linguisa*. Generally, they agreed that it tasted just fine, but after the day's events, they probably wouldn't be eating any very soon.

That day when they slaughtered the pig seemed to be a launching point for a number of life changing events.

Chapter 5

The next day, around noon, Ashley came running over to Larry's house all excited about something. He asked her what was going on.

"We're rich!" she exclaimed. "We're rich!"

"What?"

"We're rich! We got money. My mom's uncle gave us twenty-five thousand dollars!"

"Boy, how lucky," Larry said.

"Aren't you excited? I'm excited," she said breathlessly.

"I suppose."

"You suppose? You jerk. Your girlfriend is rich!"

Even at that age, Larry sensed some uneasiness with that news. He looked down at his feet and saw his big toe trying to free itself from the worn canvas sneaker. That bulging spot that was his toe was a symbol of his poor but proud status in the neighborhood. Ashley and Larry had shared those feelings, but now she had money. He was certain at that point that his proud-to-be-seen bulging toe was not quite so glamorous to someone who had just come into money.

"Say somethin'," she said.

"I don't know what to say."

"Then just say congratulations and kiss me."

He obliged her and she giggled.

"My mom says she's gonna get my teeth straightened and get my hair colored."

"What color?"

"I don't know. I'm scared about the teeth. I'll have braces."

"Braces? You mean those metal things on your teeth?"

"Yup. They'll pull my teeth around to where they should be. But don't worry; I'll be able to kiss you better."

"You can still kiss with braces on?"

"Why not? Don't you want to?"

"Sure," he said aloud, thinking to himself that it didn't sound very inviting. Ashley was the first girl he knew well who ever needed braces. The thought of placing his mouth on hers in the presence of all that metal bordered on the revolting.

"You'll still like it, you'll see," she said with a smile. She kissed him lightly then spun around and darted back to her house.

That same day, the news reported that the war in Europe was over. That meant Larry's dad would be coming home soon. Now, he was just as excited as Ashley had been over her new status. He was to discover that each of these events signaled major changes for both Ashley and him.

In less than two weeks, Ashley presented herself with her glittering new smile at Larry's house. His mom was impressed, even though she couldn't pass up the chance to tell Ashley that she probably wouldn't be able to get herself a boy friend until the braces came off, and heaven knows, that could take years.

Ashley glanced Larry's way and all they could do was smirk a little. His mom didn't know that they were already "steadies."

When they were alone, Ashley seemed a little nervous as she asked, "Wanna try it?"

"What?"

"Kissin', dummy. Wanna try it?"

There *was* genuine concern at this point. What was he expected to say? He just knew that he couldn't refuse and decided it would be better to say nothing and just react. So, he kissed her lightly. She leaned back, looked at him, and smiled. Then she kissed him firmly. Her tongue brushed his lips and even though it felt good, he couldn't return the action for fear that it would hurt his tongue on her braces. But he did return the firmness in that kiss.

"Ow," she said as she backed away. "When we press like that, the braces hurt my mouth a little."

It was almost two weeks before they kissed again. Ashley and her mom had been gone all morning and when Ashley came over after lunch, Larry was stunned. Her hair was neatly coiffed and was a dark brown-like color that he later learned was called auburn. Her hairdo reminded him of those flapper haircuts that were popular when his mom was young. Her freckles seemed less pronounced with her face surrounded by darker hair. Her green eyes shone with excitement.

"Whatcha think?" she asked.

"You're real pretty. Even more than before." It was the right thing to say. She beamed, stepped forward and planted a kiss on him that *had* to hurt her mouth.

"You're gonna have the prettiest girlfriend in the neighborhood," she said.

It was here that he experienced his first feeling of inadequacy.

Two weeks after that, Larry and a group of boys were playing a football scrimmage when Bobby Carson came running across the field toward them.

"Your dad is home!" he shouted at Larry.

Without a word, he tossed the football to Joey Martin and took off for home hurriedly.

It was quite a homecoming. His dad was looking fit and they sat around for hours listening to his stories. He was probably leaving out some gory details, but Larry was enthralled with his tales. He finally got too sleepy to go on, so he went to bed. It wasn't long before Larry heard his parents go to bed and he fell asleep to the sounds of his mother giggling (he didn't know mothers giggled) and his father moaning and groaning over something.

When he told Ashley about these night sounds, she looked puzzled. Her father had died several years before. She had no father at home, so obviously such sounds were mysterious to her.

"Wonder what they were doin'," she said.

"I think they were kissin'; you know, like we do. But maybe more than that."

That was the end of that conversation.

Ashley and Larry continued going steady and enjoyed each other's company and the varied pleasures they allowed themselves. Though their petting and fondling had reached an advanced level, they had abstained from what they realized, at age fourteen, lay ahead.

Larry's dad had been bouncing around from job to job since his discharge from the army, unable to get something permanent. This situation led up to the day when he announced that the family had to move because he had found a full time, permanent job about fifty miles away. They had no car, so they would have to impose on an uncle who drove a panel truck for a local bakery.

"Dammit! We're movin'!" Larry shouted to Ashley from across the street.

"What?"

"We're movin'. My dad's movin' us to Rhode Island."

"Rhode Island?"

"He's found himself a good job there."

"Oh, my God! That's terrible!" Ashley said as she crossed the street. "We won't be able to see each other anymore," she said as a teardrop escaped from the corner of her eye.

"Hey, we can write until we can find a way to be together again."

"How soon are you leavin'?"

"Not for a couple weeks yet."

She took his hand and they walked toward the schoolyard. "It's gonna be OK. It's just like in the war. Guys went in the army and their girlfriends waited for them. We can do that, right?"

"You wanna wait for me?"

"Of course I do, you jerk. Don't you wanna wait for me?"

"Yes, yes, I do."

She stepped around in front of him and gave him a peck on the cheek. They went around to the back of the building and began kissing. Suddenly, she groped him and slid her hand inside his pants.

"What are you doing?" he asked her. His breathing became irregular and he just knew he was blushing. Ashley giggled and confirmed his suspicions.

"You're blushin'!" she said.

As surprised as he was, he made no move to dissuade her and she continued to explore. He echoed her movements even though he knew that this could not go on. He disengaged and backed away. She cocked her head to one side and studied him.

"You don't have to stop, Larry. I don't want to stop."

With that, their bodies came together and there was no stopping this time. Afterward, Ashley looked fixedly into his eyes.

"Do you think this is love?" he asked her.

"Are you askin' me if I love you?"

"I'm thinkin' that it is; that I love you," he told her.

"Me, too," she said, and then proved it.

Their sexual "togetherness" involved only three full consummations before the time to part. They both cried that last evening. They promised to write regularly, as soon as Larry could send her a new address. The following morning, he was sitting in the back of his uncle's delivery truck, surrounded by the smell of freshly baked bread as they hurtled down the road to Rhode Island.

It was over a week before Larry's parents found an apartment of their own. In the meantime, they stayed with his dad's army buddy. He wrote to Ashley once, letting her know they were still looking for a place to live. Once in their own place, with their own address, he wrote Ashley again with the good news. Weeks passed with no response. He wrote again; and again. After three months, he should have known to give up but he still held out hope that Ashley would write.

All sorts of things went through his mind. Had he gotten her pregnant? Did she meet another boy so quickly? Then, to add more worry to those questions, his latest letter came back, marked *Return to Sender – No Forwarding Address.* He then wrote to Bobby Carson for information. His response was little help. All it really told him was that Ashley and her mom had moved to be closer to Ashley's boarding school. *Boarding school?* That was it. No further information.

He got a little more information from Joey. In response to his queries about Ashley, he said her mom had become *a real bitch* (his exact phrase) and wouldn't let Ashley associate with any of the kids in the neighborhood. She kept telling Ashley that no one there deserved her as a friend. Then they just up and moved.

That would probably explain why Ashley never answered his letters. *He didn't deserve her, either.*

Chapter 6

Although the months passed, then the years, Larry never stopped thinking of Ashley and wondering where she was. *Was she happy? Did she miss him as he did her?* Time seemed to pass so slowly; that is, until the Korean War started. He had finished high school and put in a year at trade school, and was working as an auto mechanic when that conflict broke out. He saw entry into the army as a sort of escape from an existence he found increasingly boring without Ashley.

Once through basic training, he donned his new army uniform and decided to visit Peabody before shipping overseas to Korea. Somehow, he hoped, he could find some information about Ashley's whereabouts.

He was walking from the bus stop, lugging his duffle bag, approaching the corner of Northend Street when Tony Silva came bounding out of his father's store.

"Larry! I thought that was you comin' around the corner." He stopped in front of him and pumped his hand eagerly. "Boy, is it ever good to see you. You look great!"

"It's just the uniform. How you been?"

"Good. Working for my dad in the store and doin' pretty good. You been in the army long?"

"No. I just finished basic and I have a short leave before I ship out for Korea."

"Oh, no," Tony said, "not Korea."

"That's where the action is. Have to expect it, I guess."

"You scared?"

"Nervous, maybe. Not scared. Anyone heard anything about Ashley?" he asked.

"Naw. Seems they just went to Boston or somewhere and went *poof*, like a puff of smoke. Her mother snubbed the whole damned neighborhood when they came into that money. Don't think she had a friend left by the time they took off."

"How was Ashley then?"

"Not the Ashley we knew. She got real quiet and stopped comin' around. You know how she always butted in on our games and stuff. She quit that."

"Doesn't anyone around here know anything?"

"No. Not a thing," Tony said softly.

"Damn! I sure can't go off to Boston and hope to find them. I only have ten days leave."

"Hey, you can stay here and maybe we can snoop around and find out something."

"Can't. Have to see my folks. I guess I'll have to wait until I come back."

"I'll be happy to help. Y'know, Bobby might have known somethin' more than he said, but he's in the army, too. He's in basic trainin' down in the Carolinas someplace."

"If you hear from him, tell him I'd like to know what he knows."

"Did you and Ashley have somethin' goin' on?"

"What do you mean?"

"Were you goin' steady or anythin' like that?"

"Something like that," He couldn't resist a slight smile (smirk?) when he realized that Tony and the guys probably had no idea of how intimate Ashley and he had become. "Why don't we scout out Joey and Stanley and see what's happening with them?"

"They're both workin' at the tannery. You can sure tell it when they come home. They stink to high heaven. They should be home in an hour or so."

Larry visited with Tony and his dad for most of the afternoon, and then hung out with the rest of the guys until early evening. Joey and Stanley claimed to know nothing, but as they parted, Joey hinted that Bobby might know something.

"What do you mean?" Larry asked.

"Well, I seen 'em on Ashley's porch and she was cryin' and Bobby had his arm around her shoulders."

"Bobby? Bobby and Ashley?"

"Yeah. Bobby told me she was pissed off because you didn't write like you said you would."

"But I *did* write. Did they do anything else?"

"I don't know. I didn't see them kiss or nothin'."

Joey couldn't add anything more than that, but that was enough. Larry felt outrage at the thought of his friend Bobby taking advantage of his girl, Ashley.

Seething inside, he tried to hide his emotions as he and Joey parted.

Later, at Tony's house, Tony's dad told Larry that Ashley's mom wasn't even talking to him just before they left, but didn't know why.

"Never said or did nothin' for her to act so high-hat," he said.

He spent the night at Tony's, then left in the morning for a quick jaunt to Rhode Island to say good-bye to his family.

His parents assured him that he had received no correspondence from Ashley all the while he was gone. Well, he figured, she had his address, but he didn't have hers. He had a sudden feeling of total helplessness, realizing that if she didn't make the first move, their chances of seeing each other again were pretty slim.

The thought sounded like that of a quitter, so he left home a couple of days early to return to Peabody. He was sure that somewhere he would uncover a clue as to Ashley's whereabouts. Unfortunately, he learned nothing new.

It took less than a month before Larry found himself at a processing center in Pusan, Korea.

"We're pushing them Chink bastards north again," his platoon sergeant said. "Don't get too comfortable 'cause we're gonna be completely mobile for a while. If you get a chance to use the latrine, you're one of the lucky ones. Best advice I can give ya is to shoot and run; just make sure you're runnin' north! And listen to me, dammit. I'm your platoon sergeant and I'm the closest thing you got to a mother over here!"

He was right. At least about the *shoot and run* stuff. For weeks, the unit moved northward so often that they were lucky to have time to brush their teeth.

It was near Suwon that he got his first R&R (Rest and Recreation) break for a week's rest. He had shot like hell and run like a banshee, screaming and cursing at the *enemy from the north* until he was hoarse. He didn't know for certain if he had actually killed anyone, but he felt a significant change coming over him. He asked himself why anyone would care if he shot some Chink bastard, never realizing that the Chink bastard also had a family, just as he did. A mother, father, brothers, sisters, cousins. Damn! What was this war all about, anyway?

Stretched out on a bunk, no military gear hanging off his body, he waited for sleep to assail his body and mind (thank you, God) and for a few moments of peace. Before his eyelids could close off the daylight around him, a familiar voice intruded upon this blessed solitude.

"Well, I'll be a son-of-a-bitch. It's you, ain't it?"

Larry's eyes popped open and there stood Bobby Carson. A few pounds thinner, but more handsome than he remembered him. He seemed to have filled in some of the areas previously occupied by adolescent fat with muscle.

"Always have been me," Larry responded, staring at him fixedly.

"That's a hell of a greeting. Whatcha doin' here?"

"R and R. You, too?"

"Yeah. My unit's pushin' up the east coast . . . yours?"

"West and west-central. Hope to be outta heavy fightin' soon."

"Me, too. So, how's everythin' else, the important stuff?"

"OK, I guess. Tony told me you know something about where Ashley is. That true?"

"Why do you ask?"

"Because I want to contact her."

"Why? You wanna fuck her up again?"

Larry bounded off the cot and stood toe-to-toe with him. "What the hell are you saying?"

"Look, you promised to write and never did. She fell apart. I don't know what you two were up to, but she was hurt and pissed off."

"Hurt! Pissed off? Hell, I wrote her, sent her postcards. What the hell are you talking about?

"All I know is that she didn't hear from you and she was cryin' and all that stuff."

"And from what Tony tells me, you really took advantage of her," he charged.

"Took advantage? What the hell are you talkin' about? She got horny and I porked her. Hell, you did, too, right?"

When Larry hit him, Bobby took a step or two backward and looked at him, bewildered.

"If we wasn't friends, I'd deck you. What the hell's wrong with you?" Bobby held his nose as a trickle of blood oozed slowly from the left nostril.

"Ashley was my girl, you asshole! We loved each other!"

"Oh, shit!" Bobby said. "I didn't know, but that might explain it."

"Explain what?"

"When we finished, she said somethin' like, 'That ain't it'."

Larry punched him in the chest.

"For Chrissake. Stop hittin' me, or at least let me know when it's comin'."

"You asshole. She meant that it wasn't me!"

"What?"

"We loved each other, you jerk. I didn't *pork* her. I love her. And she loves me!"

"Oh, shit! Never saw that comin'. Trust me, buddy, I didn't know."

"What did she mean by 'That ain't it'?"

"I guess it meant that I wasn't you, like you said. Who knows?"

Larry shoved him backward.

"Goddammit, quit poundin' on me! I wanna hit you back but don't know why!"

"Because you screwed the woman I love!" Larry pushed him again.

"I screwed a good friend who was upset. I didn't know she was yours!"

"Well, she is dammit. And if I could find her, I'd let her know that

I been writing and asking her for a reunion, if that's the right word."

"She didn't get your letters or anythin' else. Where'd you send 'em?"

"To Peabody. I didn't have any other address."

"She told me she never got nothin' from you. It really pissed her off."

Larry swung at him again, but this time, he felt he was venting frustration and accomplishing nothing. Bobby quickly sidestepped.

"Hit me one more time and our friendship is over, you bastard."

"Tell me where she is, or I *will* hit you again."

"Look, I'm sorry if you're ticked about this. I porked her because she was a friend who *needed* something and you know what *something* is to us guys," he said. "I didn't know until *after* that there might be somethin' goin' on with you guys."

"Oh, it was so much more than that to me," Larry said.

"Man, I'm so sorry. You an' me was best pals and Ashley was just a good piece of ass at the time, but I was sorta her hero, y'know?"

Larry couldn't help himself. He hit him again.

"Jesus Christ! I don't know why you have to keep smackin' me, but that better be the last time, or I'll deck you, real good!"

"It'll be the last time if you can tell me where she is!"

"All I know is it's someplace near Quincy."

"Quincy? Hell, that's not far from Peabody!"

"It's far enough if you don't have an address."

He shoved him again.

"Screw you, pal!" he shouted at Larry. He gave Larry a hard shove and he fell backward onto his cot. "Look me up when your brain starts workin' again!"

With that, he turned and stormed off. Larry watched him and felt like he had betrayed a friend, but then, wasn't it *he* who betrayed a friend? He got up and started pacing, wondering if he had destroyed any hope of renewing that friendship. Soon, all of that left his mind and all he could think about was that Ashley was near Quincy. When he got back there, he would look her up in the phone book and call.

It had to be her mother. She must have intercepted his mail and poor Ashley thought he had just gone off and forgotten her. *Damn! Just wait until I get back!* He thought. *There'll be hell to pay!*

His pacing continued, but rational thought dissipated into a stream of unspoken four-letter words as his anger peaked. The passage of time and the advent of hunger finally reached his conscious level of thought and he wandered off toward the mess tent for nourishment.

Chapter 7

Two weeks after his meeting with Bobby, the Korean War ended for him. His unit was walking along a levee splitting two huge rice paddies when, suddenly, the workers in the paddy pulled weapons from somewhere and opened fire on them. He felt something hit his left leg twice and when he looked down at his knee and ankle, all he could see was blood and gore. He thought of Mr. Silva's poor pig. He tried to move, but couldn't. Then the pain set in. His leg throbbed with a hot pulsating pain and he looked around for help, but saw nothing as he slipped into unconsciousness.

The next time he saw his leg it was suspended from some sort of traction device. His knee looked like it was inside a small keg of beer, all wrapped and swollen to twice the normal size. His ankle was in some sort of clamping device; there was an IV in his arm and monitors beeping all around him.

"Hey, soldier," an army medic came over and addressed him. "You gave us a real workout here. You lost a lot of blood and your leg is going to need some reconstruction. A doctor will be by soon to fill you in, but you should be just fine."

"How long?" he asked him. "How long have I been here?"

"Just a couple of days, but you're gonna be airlifted out to Japan as soon as the doc says you can handle the stress."

"Tell him . . ." he did not remember if he ever finished that sentence. The next time he woke up, he was in a military hospital in Japan.

"Where is this?" he asked of no one in particular.

A cute young nurse walked over to the bed and took his chart from where it hung at the foot of the bed. "Well, private St. Jacques, welcome back among the living." She looked at the chart, checked the monitor over his head and smiled.

"How long have I been here?" he asked her.

"You got here about two weeks ago and you've been in a coma the whole time. Would you like something to drink?"

"Yeah," he said. "How about a cold beer?"

She smiled again. "Now, that's a sign of recovery if ever I heard one."

She left briefly and returned with a small cup of ice cubes. "Closest thing to beer I could find," she said.

His mouth felt lined with cotton, absorbing all the moisture that should have been there. When he tried to swallow, his gag reflex tried to trigger into action. His lips were actually sticking to his teeth. As he sucked on that first ice cube, he fell instantly in love with this angelic creature that had fed it to him. At that moment, he couldn't recall any sensation he had experienced that had such overwhelming satisfaction.

"Aaahh!" was the only sentiment he could express.

"Now that you're awake, the doctors will be stopping by to ask questions and fill you in on your injuries."

"Can't feel my leg," he mumbled.

"You're just coming out of sedation." She pinched his toe. "Feel that?"

"A little. A little pressure."

"Good. You're going to be just fine, but your soldiering days are over."

He smiled inwardly. He felt he was performing his duty, but never did see any future in the army.

"When will . . . "

"When will the doctor be here?" She cut him off. "He's on his way, so you try to stay awake."

"What caused my coma?"

"We did. You were unconscious when you got here and the doctors decided to induce a coma due to the extensive blood loss, shock and related trauma."

He gestured for more ice and as she was placing one in his mouth, a doctor came over to the bed and began reviewing his chart. He said nothing for a moment, then smiled and looked at Larry.

"Well, except for that leg, everything's about back to normal, private. Your parents have been notified that you've come through with flying colors. In a few days, we can start you in therapy to get that leg working again. As well as it will be able to, that is."

He could have left that last part off. Larry was apprehensive and hungry.

"When can I eat?" he asked.

"We'll start you off with a cup of soup in a few hours," the nurse said, "and maybe a few crackers."

The next day he slipped back into a coma and suffered a massive infection. He reentered the world of the cognizant in a veteran's hospital outside of Boston weeks later. When he opened his eyes and looked around, his parents were in the room. His mom was reading a magazine and his dad was in his usual slumped down position in a chair, asleep.

"Hi," he said. "What are you doing in Japan?"

His mom bolted upright, dropped her magazine and called for the nurse. A matronly woman approached the bed and smiled at him.

"You're back in the states, son," his dad had revived and neared the bed.

His mom cried. His dad just teared up and acted as macho as he could. This was the start of Larry's recovery, or at least the part of it where he knew what was going on.

In the days following, the doctors explained how bullets had shattered bones in his lower left leg and foot. It was all put back together with pins and screws and when he looked down at his foot, he could see the pins holding things in place.

"The pins will be removed as soon as our infections specialist says that enough healing has taken place," his physical therapist told him the following morning.

"Infections specialist?"

"Yeah. We got a young captain here who's a real daredevil in treating infections and he saved that leg for you."

"I'll walk?"

"Reasonably well," he became solemn. "In the last war, they would have just taken it off at the knee. When you're fully healed and we start therapy, you'll have to use walking support. Once you can manage by yourself, you'll likely have to use a cane for the rest of your life. You were an auto mechanic, weren't you?"

Larry nodded.

"Well, you can be again, or take the GI Bill and go back to school to be something else."

"Will I be able to play the piano?"

"Did you play much before?"

"Not at all. I just thought maybe with all this surgery . . ."

"Good sign; a sense of humor. I think I just fell for one of the oldest vaudeville jokes still around."

"That you did. Let's get started," he said with a smile.

"In time private, in time."

"Call me Larry," he said. "They tell me that my soldiering days are over so let's forget the 'private' stuff."

"OK, Larry. You'll have to master a few special skills before we start."

"Skills?"

"Like eating and going to the bathroom without help."

His convalescence was taking longer than he had hoped and he was easily bored with the routine he faced day after day. During his therapy, he was presented with the Purple Heart and honorably discharged from the army. He remained in the hospital and in therapy with veteran status. After that, no one called him "private" anymore and that was a most welcome change.

Penny, a young nurse assigned to the floor where he was housed, used to spend time with him while he ate. She also visited early evenings after her shift was over and they became friends. On one of those evening visits, he told her all about Ashley and how crushed he was because Ashley thought he never wrote her nor cared anything about her.

"Still in love?" Penny asked.

"I suppose. Why else would I care what she thinks?"

"Well we're not that far from Quincy. Want me to try to look her up?"

"I looked her up in the phone book but haven't tried calling yet. The phone's listed to her mom and I'm sure her mom trashed my letters and she probably wouldn't let me talk to her anyway."

"Let me try. If her mother answers, I'll tell her I'm a friend from school or something. Do you know what school she went to?"

"No. When they left Peabody it was a vanishing act. I know she was supposed to be going to a boarding school somewhere around Boston, and nothing else."

"Well, if you let me, I'll try to find her, OK?"

"I'd appreciate that a lot," he said. He felt a sense of excitement at the thought that someone would go to the trouble of trying to find Ashley for him.

Penny was off on a three-day weekend and Larry was as antsy as one could get. *Was she looking this weekend or just relaxing? Would she call me if she found out anything?* He even stood at one of the windows for hours, in the off chance she would pull into the parking lot, but he didn't know what kind of car she drove. *Dummy!*

On Monday, her third day of break, Penny came into therapy as Larry was working out. When she saw him, eyes met briefly, and then her face virtually exploded into a smile that shook him to his toes. He grabbed firmly onto the handrails and held himself, hoping he wouldn't just collapse with all the excitement.

"I found her!" she beamed. "She's at Boston College!"

"How the hell?" he could barely contain himself.

She took him firmly by the arm. "Here. You better sit down before you fall down."

After he sat, she told him that she had called the Cummings phone number and talked to Ashley's mom.

"I told her I found her wallet in a diner and wanted to return it to her."

"She believed that?"

"Yes, and all she could talk about was what a stupid little girl she had raised. She said she couldn't believe she had gotten into college and the fact that she had lost her wallet was evidence that college wasn't doing her that much good."

"Never cared for that woman when I was a kid and I surely can't stand her now."

Penny paused and looked at him seriously. "I know you didn't ask me to, but I called Ashley."

"You called her?"

"Yes. She seemed confused when I told her where you were."

"Good Lord, I'll have to call her and explain why I didn't call her myself."

"Well, this number is one of those dorm numbers. You never know who's going to answer and, well, she asked me not to give you the number."

"What? Oh, man, she must really be pissed at me if she doesn't even want to talk."

"I don't know about that," Penny said. Then she smiled and added, "She felt you should meet and talk. She's arranging to be here sometime Friday."

With that, he understood that trite literary expression *I was beside myself,* for never before had he experienced such anxiety, excitement and hope all wrapped up together.

Penny took his arm and they walked to the lunchroom. Well, she walked. He still hobbled.

Chapter 8

The Tuesday to Friday until Ashley's visit was the longest four-day period in his total existence. Each day seemed longer than the last. When Friday came, he was awake early and spent an hour trying to make himself presentable. He remembered how shabbily shod he was when they were last together and as he looked down at his G.I. slippers, he couldn't help but smile. Maybe he could manage to poke his right toe through the top of the slipper to be more in character; at least as close to how he was when they were steadies. He chuckled to himself.

It was mid-afternoon before Ashley arrived. Larry was waiting in the dayroom when Penny bounded in, smiling. "She's here," she said. "She's gorgeous! I sat her at a table in the lounge where you can have a little bit of privacy. Come on." She pulled on his arm, but it didn't take much effort until he was on his feet, leaning heavily on his cane, making his way. Penny left him at the entrance to the lounge and he approached Ashley slowly.

She looked at his cane and watched him take a few careful steps. Then she looked up into his eyes and smiled. "I hear you've had a rough time," she said.

"Now that you're here, I would gladly go through it again." He sat across from her.

"Penny tells me that you wrote me like you said you would."

"Yes. I was crushed when you didn't answer."

"I even thought once that my mom was behind that, but I hoped she wouldn't be *that* mean."

He didn't just look at her; he devoured her with his eyes. She was stunning. Her auburn hair was still short and she had only a hint of makeup. Some of her freckles still managed to decorate her face. Her smile was a classic array of straight, white teeth.

"No more braces." he observed aloud.

"No. I just wear a retainer at night."

"Are you seeing anyone?"

"Not steady," she said. "You were the last one of those. And you? Are you and Penny . . . you know?"

"Oh, no. Penny's just a good friend. We talk a lot and one night I told her about us."

"You told her about the sex?"

"Lord, no, Ashley. That was ours. Just for us to know about. I told her about the silly games we played and about Mr. Silva's pig and, well, how I came to love you."

"I often wondered," Ashley began, "if what we felt was love or if it was just the sex. Of course, when I doubted you for not writing, I doubted everything about you; about us. And I have to be honest, I'm truly confused and don't know if we have anything now. I had to get on with things and my mom sure wasn't going to let me dwell on the loss. So I got to work forgetting you."

"I'm so sorry," he told her. "You have to know now that I didn't mean for anything like that to happen."

"Well, finishing school took all the childhood crap out of me and replaced it with something they called decorum."

The small talk was wearing thin on his patience. He wanted to pull her to him and hug for all he was worth, but there was a lump in his throat and pressure in his chest that seemed to immobilize him.

"How long are you going to be here?" Ashley asked.

"Almost done," he answered. "When they discharge me, I'll have to come in here or wherever for more therapy; maybe for another year or two."

"God, what happened to you?"

"My leg was shattered and they had to rebuild it. I've got rods and screws holding it all together. I can't bend my leg much and my ankle is virtually immobile. But I made it and a lot of my buddies didn't."

"And we thought the war when we were kids was the last one, remember?"

"Yeah. But that's not all I remember when we were kids. We had something special, Ashley. There was a magic that we need to capture again."

"I know. Recapturing it may be difficult. We're different people now."

"Don't go all logical on me, Ashley. For me, the magic is still there. It never went away. I know we can have that again."

"I wish I could be that sure of it. Let's face it; we have to get reacquainted again. Neither of us is what we were."

"I understand, Ashley," he reached out and took her hand, "but for me that magic is still in my heart. If I have to work at restoring that for you, I'm ready. If that means getting reacquainted, then let's start there."

"You know," Ashley smiled, "I'm the one who got all that decorum stuff and, according to the teachers, I really matured into something different than what I was. But the way you're talking, you've done some maturing, too."

"When you watch friends die, lying in the mud, it tends to change your outlook on a lot of things. But when I thought I had seen enough to go nuts, I always found a level of sanity thinking of you and what we had meant to each other."

Ashley smiled. "If you're trying to make me blush, it won't work. After you left and there was no mail, I did a few things I'm not proud of."

"I know about Bobby," he said. They just sat and stared at each other.

"How the hell?"

"I ran into Bobby when we were on R&R in Korea. He told me."

Her face reflected her anger, much like the thunderclouds that foretell violent weather. Her visage voiced an unspoken question: *How could he?*

"It wasn't like that. He wasn't boasting or anything like that. He honestly felt he had done something honorable."

"Honorable? What a jerk! He actually thought he was doing something honorable?"

Larry knew they had entered into an area where most sensible men would realize there was a minefield ahead. He considered himself a sensible man.

"That's not important," he said reassuringly. "What we did and who with doesn't change what we had."

"Bull shit," she responded. *"I'm sorry for that.* That's something we were taught to say whenever we made a crass remark. He never should have told anyone. Did you tell anyone about us?"

"No, Ashley, but how did Bobby know we had sex?"

"Oh, shit! *I'm sorry for that.* I guess it was something I said."

"It's not important. What went on after your mother intercepted my letters was distorted by misinformation."

"But Bobby wasn't the only one."

"Good Lord, Ashley, I don't care. How many more?" he added.

"From what you're saying, it doesn't matter, right?"

"Well, yeah, I guess. Was it a lot?"

"Do you really want to know?"

"That many?"

"No, not many; only a few. But I thought you didn't care, you jerk."

"But I did. Every day, every night, all I thought about was you. And I have to confess, the magic of the sex we had, the few times we had it, was all I could remember."

"Either you're a total romantic, or horny as hell."

"Guilty," he said.

"We're warming up, aren't we?"

He looked at her. He still wanted to pull her close and squeeze the life out of her. All he could muster up was a smile. He had reached a point where he thought anything else he might say would blow him out of the water. A pregnant moment of silence ensued.

"Well," she began, "I have a long drive ahead of me. Maybe I can come back next weekend and we could drive some place. How often do you get out of here?"

"Not often," he told her. "Not much reason to go anywhere."

"Penny doesn't take you out?"

"Just on the grounds. I told you we didn't have anything going."

"How long has it been since you had a good hamburger?"

"Define good. We have hamburgers here a couple of times a week."

"It's my treat. I know where we can get a hamburger that's sinful! You'll have to get a weekend pass if there is such a thing, because it's too far to drive there and back in one day. We can stay at my place before the return trip."

He listened and his heart continued to thump in his chest with the consistency of a base drum in a marching band. He had held a fear within that their first meeting would actually be the introduction to the end of the relationship, but this would seem to be the renewal of the magic they had known.

"Can you get cheese and pickles on it?" he asked. He just couldn't think of anything more profound to say.

"You can have anything on it that you want," she said with a smile.

"When?"

"I'll pick you up Saturday morning. Be ready by ten."

"I'll be a basket case until then," he said.

She hadn't been gone ten minutes before he thought of a dozen other things he wished he had said to her. He was excited about the coming weekend. Maybe the magic was still there for both of them.

Shortly after Ashley left, Penny came into the lounge and approached.

"So how'd it go, Larry? Are you OK?"

He looked up at her and smiled. He gestured that she should sit, and she did so.

"What are you still doing here?" he asked her. "You're not even on duty today."

"I just wanted to be sure everything went OK," she said.

"It did," he said, unable to control the smile that lit up his face. "We're going for a hamburger, come Saturday."

"Oh, my God," Peggy said with a chuckle. "That's so romantic."

"Yuk, yuk, yuk. I was afraid there would be nothing for me beyond this meeting, and I have to add that I really appreciate your finding her and getting her to come here to see me."

"What are friends for?" She arched her eyebrows, making them serve as marks of punctuation. Then she smiled and added, "I can't think of anyone else I would rather do something like that for."

"I'm eternally grateful," he said.

She didn't respond; that is, she didn't *say* anything in response. Her expression, however, posed some interesting questions for Larry. She actually looked like there was something magical between *them.* Her eyes had softened and she looked just like Ashley did when they first explored their love for each other. *Good grief,* he thought, *was this another magical moment he would have to contend with?*

In an attempt to handle what was an awkward moment, he muttered, "I mean, only one hell of a good friend would do this for a guy she barely knows."

"Sure, sure. I've got to get out of here. See you tomorrow."

He continued to sit there, wondering what Saturday held in store. For the rest of that week, he thought of little else.

Larry rose with the sun on Saturday and was all spruced up by eight o'clock. He remembered his mom's favorite expression, *nervous as a kitten*. It certainly could be used to describe him that morning. When Ashley arrived, he wanted to lunge at her and sweep her up in a hug that would express exactly how he felt, but she hadn't warmed up to him enough for that yet.

It was great being away from the rehab center. He realized that in the months he had been there, he hadn't ventured out but once or twice. Ashley was driving an old but neat little convertible, top down, cruising along at about sixty. He was absolutely, completed elated. She drove and drove, and soon he saw a sign for Boston College. Next was the sign welcoming them to Chestnut Hill. Ashley had driven all the way back to the college for that hamburger break.

"Holy cow," he said. "We didn't have to come this far for a burger."

"For my burger, we did," she said with a smile. "I share a small apartment with a girlfriend, but she's gone home for the weekend, so I thought we could have that hamburger in my kitchen. I make a hell of a burger, trust me."

His heart quickened. The thought of being alone with her brought more to his mind than a hamburger, but he realized that was so much foolishness. He tried to focus on succulent, red meat, sizzling in a frying pan; it seemed to work. His stomach growled in anticipation.

She wheeled into a parking lot and took the first available parking slot. They got out of the car and went to the door of a basement apartment. Ashley deftly opened it and walked through. He followed, saying nothing. She went directly to the kitchen and began fussing with the tools and the ingredients that would result in their lunch. There was much small talk and he noticed a hi-fi set in the corner. As Ashley prepared lunch, he looked through a short stack of LPs and realized that Ashley was into big band swing. He selected a disc by Jimmy Dorsey and placed it on the turntable. By the time it got to the fourth band, the burgers were ready. Ashley was right; she made a hell of a burger.

They ate in silence while the music played. Then Ashley broke into the musical interlude with, "You like swing?"

"Sure," he answered. "After all, we grew up with it. What's not to like?"

"There's a courtyard on the other side of the building. Why don't we go sit for a while and catch up."

"Fine," he said, "but I don't know that there's much more catching up to do, except for some small talk."

"What's wrong with small talk?"

"Nothing, as long as it's with you."

"Are you trying to turn on the old St. Jacques charm?"

"Not intentionally, but I would like to hold you and to tell you I still love you."

They sat next to each other on a bench in the courtyard. They were close enough that he was able to put his arm around her. She moved closer, saying, "We have all night to talk about all that, if it's still there."

Talk about confusion! He was thrilled about staying all night, but concerned with that "if it's still there" line.

Chapter 9

They spent the evening talking about their childhoods and the fun they had together. They shared more laughs over the fate of Mr. Silva's poor pig than anything else. When they talked about their discovery of each other, the talk became more serious and led up to a night of lovemaking that triggered every known "happy response" that exists in the human condition. Larry thought he had read it somewhere, but the phrase that best fit was "deliriously happy."

It was the middle of the afternoon on Sunday when Ashley brought him back to the rehab center. Penny was on duty and greeted them at the door.

"Welcome back, you two," Penny said smiling. "How'd the leg hold up Larry?"

"Pretty good. I'm supposed to get out of here in a week or two and for the first time, I feel ready to fly the nest."

"I expected to have to help him more than I did," Ashley said, "but he was pretty self-sufficient."

They went into the lounge and made small talk for about an hour. Penny stayed for part of the time, but had duties to perform, so she was in and out. When it was time for Ashley to go, they embraced warmly.

"Walk me to the door?"

"I'll just sit here for a while, remembering how wonderful last night was."

She smiled, kissed him on the forehead and turned to go. "I'll say goodbye to Penny on my way out."

"When will I see you again?"

His words fell on empty space as Ashley swished through the doorway. He sat back down and he just knew he had a whimsical little smile on his face. After the night he had just experienced, he was certain he would hear from her again, and soon.

It was too soon. The next morning Penny handed him an envelope.

"Ashley asked me to give you this," she said.

He didn't want to take it from her. There was something ominous looking about that envelope. It looked like a simple envelope, but he knew that the contents couldn't be anything for which he was hoping. *Why would she just leave me* that, *whatever it was?* He forced himself to open it as Penny discreetly walked away. He removed the sheet of paper inside and unfolded it. It was as he feared.

> *Dear Larry,*
>
> *I can't tell you how nice it was to get back together. I was so excited about being with you again, hoping that the magic was still there, as you put it. I think that the magic, though, was the stuff of our childhood. There was physical pleasure for me, but nothing like that which we knew as kids and certainly not enough for us to consider getting serious again. I can only hope you find happiness and regain full use of your leg. You will always be among my fondest memories.*
>
> *Ashley*

He didn't know how many times he had read it through. *The stuff of our childhood? Physical pleasure?* Those two phrases filled his head with harsh noise like that of clanging bells. Hell, he even told her he still loved her and had never stopped.

How could she reduce what we had to the stuff of our childhood *and* physical pleasure?

He crumpled the letter and the envelope in his hand, looking around for a place to dump it; no, *throw* it. He spent the rest of that day sulking. His demeanor must have sent up some sort of signal because no one said much to him during the day. Even Penny seemed to be avoiding him and that made him wonder if she had some foreknowledge of the contents of that envelope.

When she finally came in before leaving, he said to her, "Did you know what was in the envelope?"

"No," she said. "I figured it wasn't good news. That doesn't usually come in an envelope dropped off with a friend."

"Hell, I'm thinking back over the time we spent together and don't know when she found the time to write it, brief though it was."

"She's got someone else?"

"Don't know," he said. "She didn't mention anyone. Just said the magic wasn't there anymore. At least not for her."

"I'm so sorry. I don't know what else to say."

"Nothing else *to* say. It's over and probably it's a good thing. I wouldn't want a one-sided relationship. That would be too selfish."

"You're pretty calm about it."

"I sulked all day and it didn't change anything. I guess I really lost her way back then, when I left Peabody. I wrote, but her mother obviously saw to it that Ashley never got the letters. It's not easy, trying to see it from Ashley's point of view, but she has no real feel for how I felt during those years when we didn't see each other. Hell, she even had sex with one of my buddies."

"You can't blame her for that," Penny said. "She was hurt, vulnerable and in need of affection."

"Yeah. So was I."

"Well, I have to go. We can talk some more tomorrow if you want."

"Yeah, maybe. See you."

Penny left and he sat staring at the empty doorway.

"Hey, Larry," another patient called, "chow's on. You eatin'?"

He got up and walked along to the center's cafeteria. *Damn! They were serving hamburgers!*

He was discharged shortly after Ashley's farewell and through the VA placement service, he got a decent job as the service manager at a nearby Chevy dealership. As a mechanic, he had specialized in carburetors and the knowledge he had gained played a role in his rapid advancement. Although the job title didn't change, the salary did and he found himself living comfortably in a small, but efficient apartment near downtown. Even with his bum leg, it was a short and easy walk.

He had been there for almost a year when one morning, Penny drove in for routine service on her car.

"Well aren't you looking well," she said as Larry approached her.

They were both smiling as she got out of her car. They gave each other a healthy hug. "You're looking pretty good yourself," he said softly into her ear.

"I didn't know if you were still in this job when I called to schedule my car in, but I had hoped so. It's so good to see you again."

"And you," he answered. "I can't believe we haven't kept in touch. After all, we became more than patient and nurse. We were good friends."

"Were you waiting for me to reach out first?" she asked.

"That probably wouldn't have been a good idea, you know, the old nurse stalking her ex-patient."

"Old?" she asked with arched eyebrows.

"Oops. I meant a past nurse; a one-time nurse; definitely not old."

She laughed and as they exchanged information on her car, he filled out the service order and scheduled her for the next available mechanic. The time needed to complete the servicing on the car would bring them right around lunchtime, so he asked her if they could lunch together at a small café a few doors down from the dealership.

"I'd love to," she said. "It'll be great to get caught up."

At lunch, Larry looked at her across the table as she rambled on about how things were going at the hospital, updating him on the staff and about the internal politics of the operation. Then, adding seamlessly into that conversation she inserted, "You seeing anyone?"

Slightly taken aback, he smiled a little and said, "No. Are you?"

"No," she said with a smile. He sensed she was pleased with his answer. "I go to dinner once in a while and maybe a lunch here or there, but there's no one who could qualify as 'being involved with.' You are dating, though, aren't you?"

"Oh, I flirt with waitresses and cashiers. I've been out to dinner once or twice and to a movie now and then, but always with different people. I'm beginning to think I must be boring to them. We exchange numbers, but neither of us calls."

"I can't believe that!" she exclaimed. "You have to be the least boring person I know. That didn't come out right," she quickly added. "I mean *I* never found you boring, how could they?"

"Maybe they just read me; could see a lack of interest."

"Really? You're not *interested* in women?"

"Now there's another thing that didn't come out right."

They laughed and she reached for his hand and held it across the small table. It felt warm and comfortable. They had held hands before, but she was usually helping him get up, sit down or walk when he was recovering. This time, he could feel the friendship in the clasp of hands.

He looked at her seriously and asked, "Are you suggesting that we start dating?"

She blushed. "Pretty obvious, wasn't I? It's just that I think of you often and I really miss you. I think it would be real nice if we could at least see each other now and then."

"I don't know how to handle this. Isn't the guy supposed to make the first move?"

"Only if the girl is patient enough to wait for him to get around to it."

"You realize that I'm under no obligation to please you since you asked first."

"Good grief, Larry. I'm not asking you to marry me."

"And you better not. If it comes to that, *I* will do the asking."

"Now my heart is all a-flutter."

"Mine, too, I think. I'm not sure what 'aflutter' means."

"My car should be ready. We better go." She reached for her purse.

"This is on me," he said.

They left the café and strolled back to the dealership. About half way back, somehow they were holding hands. He wasn't sure who initiated that, and he didn't think Penny knew, either.

They dated regularly, but it wasn't until they were both celebrating birthdays that they had their first sexual experience with each other.

Larry couldn't honestly compare it to what he had learned to accept as the *childhood magic* he had known with Ashley, but it was more meaningful to him than any previous experience since then. Their relationship continued and intensified and one night as they were lying beside each other she said, "I have to ask you something."

"Me first," he interjected. "Will you marry me?"

She started to laugh. "Yes, but that's not what I was going to ask you."

He pulled her atop him and whispered, "Later."

Afterward as they snuggled together, he asked, "What were you going to ask me?"

She laughed. "Should I sell my car and get a new one?"

"Let's wait and see how much the wedding's going to cost."

In just over three months, they had everything arranged and were married in a quiet, little ceremony in a chapel adjacent to a local catholic church. Several of Penny's friends from the hospital were there, her parents came up from New Jersey and his folks came in from Rhode Island. Bobby and Tony also showed up at the chapel.

"What are you guys doing here?" Larry asked them.

"We came for the wedding, dummy. Penny contacted us. We didn't know who she was but when she said she was marrying you, we dropped everything to be here," Tony said.

"I hope you don't mind that I came," Bobby said a little sheepishly.

"Why should I?"

"Well, last time we saw each other you pounded on me pretty good."

"Oh, that. No matter now, buddy. I've moved past that."

"Me, too. Got myself a steady and we'll probably get married as soon as I get out of the army . . . if I get out. I was supposed to be in for three years and hoped I could get out when the war ended, but now I'm even thinking I might stay for a career."

"And what about you, Tony?" Larry asked.

"My dad's leaving me the store, so I'm going to stay right there on Northend Street, I guess. Been dating a couple of girls, but no sure thing yet."

"Man, it seems like Northend was so long ago. I guess what happens to a guy in a war makes him feel older than he is."

Bobby silently nodded.

The wedding and reception was over by six that evening. Penny and Larry went off to Cape Cod for a three-day weekend, the only honeymoon they could afford.

Penny had moved in with him a week before the wedding. He had the lower rent. Once settled in after a brief honeymoon, Penny came up with the idea to sell her car for a newer one with an automatic transmission so that Larry could drive again. He hadn't driven or even attempted to, since returning from Korea. The idea appealed to him, so they did it and he was driving again in short order. With the new car came a new freedom. They drove to see her folks in New Jersey, to see his folks in Rhode Island, and his boyhood pals in Peabody.

Penny and Larry were blissfully happy and they decided that it was time to start a family. He jokingly told her he didn't know how that was done, but she promised to help. Now their sexual activity was not merely for physical pleasure; they were working toward a family. He had no idea at the time, how difficult that was going to be.

Chapter 10

They were approaching their fifth anniversary and Penny still had not conceived. Her doctor friends at the VA hospital told her it was not uncommon for combat veterans to have some problems of this nature when they returned home. They told her that they still didn't fully understand how trauma affected the psyche of veterans. Even a leg wound like Larry's could lead to all sorts of reactions they were hard pressed to explain. Their advice was to just relax and enjoy each other. They advised that conception would occur when things were right.

The "just relax" prescription didn't work, but Penny and Larry were really enjoying each other. Some of the things they tried were downright comical, but supposedly worked for some people. Penny drank some of the weirdest concoctions because they were supposed to improve fertility. She stood on her head immediately after sex. She used warm compresses before and after sex. She took all kinds of natural herbal supplements. Then, one day she just stopped.

"I'm done," she said. "I love you Larry, and I do want a baby with you. And I'm sure I will when all the stars align or whatever the hell is supposed to make conception possible."

"The doctor at the VA said he knew of a program," Larry said.

"I know. I talked with him. They call it a fertility clinic and they analyze my eggs and your sperm. Confidentially, I don't care if you have what they call 'lazy sperm.' Let's leave it to Mother Nature, OK?

Besides those new clinics are all about making big money; money we don't have."

"I did want to get you pregnant, honey and I really tried. I'm so sorry."

"Trying is all we can do. Maybe if we just quit trying, it'll happen. I've heard of that happening before."

"Maybe. But I'll never stop loving you, no matter what," he assured her.

"I know that, silly," she said, "and when I said to quit trying, I didn't mean to quit sex, OK?"

"Absolutely. How about now?"

"You're an animal," she said as she approached him seductively.

Stars hadn't aligned after a month of "casual, whenever they wanted to" sex; nothing had changed. Then, Penny floored him.

"Let's adopt," she said. No prelude, no mention of it leading up to that statement. "The church has a program going with a Korean orphanage and we could probably get a baby or at least a little guy."

Wow. A little guy. She even had decided on a boy before mentioning it.

"What?" After reaching deep down into the mental recesses of his sometimes-feeble mind, that was the most profound statement he could make. *Way to go, Larry!*

"Adopt," she said half smiling. "You know what that is, don't you? Like making a home for a little person who has no parents?"

"Of course I know what that is. Are you sure? Have you thought it all out?"

"Been mulling it over for weeks and talked to Father O'Malley briefly last Sunday. He said we were naturals and could easily adopt."

"If you're sure, we can talk to him some more and see what happens."

She lunged at him and wrapped her arms around his neck.

Larry thought he was under attack for something until she squealed, "I love you! I was so afraid you wouldn't want to upset this *tea for two* arrangement."

"Why would you think that? As hard as I tried to get you pregnant, you should have considered this an easy sell."

"Adoption, maybe; it's the Korean thing I thought you might balk at."

"The war's been over for a while. I doubt there are any more infants in the orphanages."

"Yeah. That's the other thing. It would have to be at least a two year old."

"You really have dug into this, huh? You really want it?"

"Yes. We have so much love to share, why don't we do it with someone who really needs us?"

"OK," he said, "let's do it."

She giggled and began nibbling on his ear. He wondered if the stars were about to align.

It didn't take long for them to find a cute little two-year-old boy, but by the time they satisfied all the bureaucratic requirements and passed all the "suitable parents" tests, their son was suddenly a three-year-old. Several months after that they went to Korea with help from the church to pick up their treasure, now legally renamed Moru St. Jacques.

"What a hell of a combo," he told Penny. "The poor kid will have to grow up with an Oriental first name and a French surname."

"The name doesn't matter. Besides, his father was an American G.I. He'll be ours and that will make him something special."

"We should have given him a new legal first name, too," Larry said.

When they arrived at the orphanage, they entered the front entrance, greeted by the Mother Superior. Holding her hand was the cutest little toddler they had ever seen. Larry had some strange feelings about being in Korea again. The reconstruction was under way and everything seemed brighter than before, during the war. The trees seemed greener, the sky bluer and everyone seemed so upbeat and pleasant. Any weird feelings were gone the instant he looked into those dark smiling eyes. The little guy was obviously coached. His grin split his face horizontally and it looked like it could even hurt; obviously forced.

Penny gave a little whimper of some sort and stretched out her arms. Moru rushed to her and as they embraced, his forced smile turned into a beam of natural sunshine, his eyes sparkling. She nearly collapsed when he looked into her eyes and said, "Hi, mama." The sisters obviously left little to chance with these meetings. Penny hugged him so hard Larry was afraid she might hurt him. "Hi, Moru," she said, all choked up.

Larry was surprised at how smoothly everything went from that point on. Moru knew exactly what was going on and was obviously thrilled with it. His English was limited at best, but he made valiant efforts to be understood. Penny observed that his face was so easy to read, language would prove to be no insurmountable barrier.

The trip home was uneventful. They were happy to note that Moru was fully potty-trained and showed signs that he would soon be proficient in all aspects of his toilet training. He delighted in the smallest gifts and thoroughly enjoyed being the center of attention.

Penny took him to the hospital to show off and the strangest thing happened. Several of the veterans there, still confined to extensive therapy programs, seemed to connect somehow to this little Korean-American toddler. They showered him with candy, simple toys and enjoyed playing with him when he visited. Doctors told Penny that Moru had a therapeutic affect on the patients and welcomed him whenever he could visit. One soldier, Private Jim Kohn, who had great difficulty *walking the rails*, was surprised one day when Moru squealed with pleasure and applauded as only a three-year old can, when he made it to the end of the rails. He smiled at Moru and said, "Again?"

"Again, again," Moru repeated the word and laughed. The soldier negotiated the rails again with seemingly more energy than the first time.

One afternoon, Penny was looking for Moru to put him down for a nap. She found him with Jim. Moru's head was resting on Jim's chest and he was blissfully asleep. Jim appeared to be drowsy, too. He looked up and smiled at Penny. "I've got him," he said.

This arrangement was saving Penny and Larry a good chunk of cash they would have been spending on baby sitters. Unfortunately, some of it was hard on Moru. He couldn't understand when Jim left the hospital. They were buddies, after all. Jim went home to his parents in Worcester, never to return to the rehab center.

It was a surprise on Moru's fourth birthday when a knock on the door preceded Jim's entry into the house, bearing gifts for Moru. For over an hour, Moru studied Jim, as if to assure that it was indeed his buddy from the hospital. Then he warmed to the situation. This was a birthday he would remember for years to come.

They heard from Jim two or three more times on Moru's birthdays, but somewhere along the way they lost touch. Moru, of course, was growing strong and healthy and had adapted to school quite nicely. He still visited the hospital on non-school days, but he never got quite as close to anyone as he had to Jim.

"Do you think we should adopt again?"

Penny had this way of popping significant questions when least expected. Larry gaped.

"Why? Isn't Moru a big enough handful? He just goes to school, you know. It's not like he's off exploring the universe."

"Oh, I know, but actually, I'm thinking of Moru. Sometimes I think he might be lonely and how nice it would be for him to have a little sister."

"How could he be lonely? He has us and all his buddies at the hospital. The kid is bombarded with love every day."

"He's going to outgrow that soon, Larry. The patients love little kids, but what happens as he matures?"

"Wow. Do you think it's time I bought him his first razor?"

"Don't make fun of me. Let's just leave the subject for now; there's plenty of time to figure out what we want to do."

"Whatever. I didn't have a clue you were going to come up with that."

"I'm exciting, huh?" She smiled and winked.

"Mildly put." he smiled in return.

Later that evening, she said, "Wanna sleep on it?"

"What?"

"Another adoption," she said.

"I would like to wait until we know just what we can afford. Were you thinking another Korean?"

"Not necessarily. What do you think?"

"Not thinking about anything, really. I'm not sure I'm ready for it. Are you?"

She stared at him intently. "Not ready for what; another adoption or another Korean?"

"Oh, hell. I didn't mean that. Moru's a delight and if we can get another one like him, well, you know what I mean."

"But a nice American kid would be nice, too, wouldn't it?"

"Yeah, but it doesn't matter. It's just that I haven't given further adoption a thought. Obviously, you've been thinking about it."

"Not like the last time," she said. "Actually, I was just wondering how you felt about it and you don't seem to favor the idea."

"We haven't considered the idea until now."

"True," she said. Then she smiled and added, "Maybe we should just mull it over for a while and see what we come up with."

"You mean shift gears?"

"That's up to you. If you want to do it, so do I, but I don't want you to feel pressured."

"You know that's a joke. I want to please you so much, just knowing you want it creates pressure."

She walked to him and sat in his lap. "Let's relieve the pressure and you can stop worrying about it. There's no time limit."

"You sure know how to change the subject."

"Just one of my feminine wiles."

"Wile away," he said and they kissed.

The subject of another adoption seemed to hang in limbo for months and, after over a year, no further mention of it had occurred. Moru continued to grow and mature and he was truly an all-American boy, involved in most school sports and excelling in most of his subjects.

"Why do they teach genetics in school?" Moru asked one evening as he was doing his homework. "All the kids in my class have genes from their parents, but I don't; so, what do I care about whose genes do what?"

Larry smiled and said, "You don't have genes from us, but your genes surely came from your own parents."

"But who are they? Why does it matter? I have the good life right here and I wouldn't change it for nothin'. You guys *are* my parents."

Larry walked up behind his chair, bent down and gave him a hug.

"C'mon, dad," he said, "don't get sloppy."

Chapter 11

Larry expected the subject of another adoption would come up again, but it never did. He assumed that Penny felt he wasn't all in favor of it, and he wasn't so sure himself. He decided to defer to her and perhaps she was deferring to him. In any event, it seemed there would be no further adoptions if he didn't initiate the thought. He never got around to it. But then, he didn't have to. The "thought" materialized in the strangest way.

At the time, the nation was embroiled in another military action (not a war) in Viet Nam. Political shenanigans, battle casualties and body counts filled the daily news accounts and it was weird watching a war on their living room television. Penny and Larry were apolitical, but Moru became fascinated with the daily accounts, studied newspapers and looked into the history of Viet Nam.

"Did you know that we have been messing with Viet Nam since 1954?" Moru asked after the evening news.

"Really?" Larry responded.

"Yeah. We put up some prince to rule South Viet Nam and there was supposed to be an election in 1954. Ho Chi Minh looked like the winner, so we stopped it."

"I'm sure it's more complicated than that," Larry said.

"Maybe, but I think it's just like Korea, but there was no election set for there."

"Is that so?"

"Yeah. It's really all about 'spheres of influence' for us, Russia and China. It's that old Communism stuff. I have a lot more to read up on it."

"Why such an interest?" Larry asked him.

"I'm more interested in the history, I think. I think war is just the result of dumb politics."

"Ah, the old 'failures in diplomacy' theory."

"Huh?"

Before Larry could answer, the doorbell rang and he got up to answer it. When he opened the door, he stood dumbfounded. His knees grew weak as he gazed into the pretty, green eyes of Ashley! Ashley, as gangly as girls get. She had skinny, little girl legs, with knees that were already adult-sized. She had elbows so sharp; she could have probably punctured a coconut with them to get at its milk. She wore her red-orange hair short. Not so wise for someone who had ears like Dumbo's. And there were the freckles, where angels kissed her when she was a baby; kissed her a lot!

With his mind in a whirl, all he could do was nod in response to her question: "Are you Laurent St. Jacques? I'm Ashley's daughter. She said you would understand this." She thrust an envelope at him. He took it from her, opened it and viewed its contents in stunned silence.

It was a birth certificate for Ashleigh Cummings. Ashley was listed as the mother; the word "unknown" was listed as the father. He looked back at her, then noticed the small note attached to the document. It read: *Ash, it's time you knew. Your father's name is Laurent St. Jacques.* He looked down at the small suitcase next to her on the floor. He looked back into her eyes and noticed tears were welling up.

"You're my father," she whispered.

"So it would seem," he said. *What a stupid response. Way to go, Larry!*

What followed was awkward to say the least, but he found himself leaning over and embracing this reincarnation of his Ahsley!

"My mom's dead. She told me to find you because she didn't want me staying with gramma. She told me things."

"Come in," he said. "You can tell me everything."

As they entered, Moru stood and looked at Ashleigh. She merely looked back.

"Moru," Larry began, "this is your half-sister Ashleigh. Ashleigh, this is Moru."

Ashleigh looked at him and said, "You're oriental."

"Yeah."

"Moru, go tell your mother to come in. She's in the kitchen." To Ashleigh he asked, "Have you eaten?"

"No. I came here right from the bus station. Mom gave me your address and once I got off the bus, all I wanted to do was get here."

"You traveled all alone?" Larry asked.

"Mom told me it was better if I just high-tailed it as soon as I could."

Penny entered the living room and broke into a broad smile. "Oh my God, it's Ashleigh," she said. Then, more solemnly, "Your mom? The leukemia?"

Ashleigh nodded as tears welled up once again.

"Wait a minute," Larry said to Penny, "you knew about this?"

Penny took a deep breath. "Yes. Ashley contacted me a few months ago because all her treatments had failed and she didn't have much time left. She swore me to secrecy, but admitted that she was worried about your daughter. So, I told her not to worry and that we would take good care of her."

"How could you not tell me?"

"I promised Ashley; it was what she wanted. She was dying, Larry. I couldn't refuse her."

Larry looked at Ashleigh and noted that the tears now were running down her cheeks as she cried in silence. Something in him recognized that she needed some reassurance, acceptance.

"We can discuss this later. First, Ashleigh, you are more than welcome here. If you want to make this your home, with us, we'd be happy to arrange it. But, Penny, this young lady is hungry. Why don't you and Moru go see what kind of a meal you can rustle up for her."

"You bet," Moru said, "there's a couple chicken legs left."

Penny and Moru went into the kitchen. Larry took Ashleigh's hand and led her to the couch where they sat next to each other.

"Now, Ashleigh, you have a story to tell and I'm anxious to hear it. Did your mother have a nickname for you?"

"She called me 'Ash' unless she was mad at me. Then she called me

Ashleigh. Gramma thought it was silly to have the same names. That's why mine is spelled different."

"Did she tell you why you should come right over here when she died?"

"She didn't want me to be with gramma because she always called me 'the bastard'."

Larry was stunned to think that a grandmother could use such a name for her own grandchild. "She told me once that you raped my mother and made her a whore, but I'm not even sure what that means. My mom told me you were childhood sweethearts and that you were in love. What happened?"

Larry told her how he wrote and that he thought her grandmother had thrown his letters away.

"So your mom thought I didn't care about her after I moved and we didn't see each other until I came home from Korea. Penny was my nurse and she found your mom and got us back together; for a weekend anyway."

"Mom told me that's when you made me."

Larry thought he was blushing, wondering what to say to that when Penny rescued him by parading in with Moru, holding a plate of food. Moru was carrying a glass of milk.

"Come over to the table and dig in, honey," Penny said.

Dig in, she did. During her assault of the chicken legs, the phone rang. Answering it, Larry was surprised to hear the greeting from the other end.

"Ah, Mr. St. Jacques, my daughter's rapist!"

"What?"

"This is Ashley Cummings' mother. Is your little bastard child safely at home with you now?"

"How dare you? She's a beautiful child and of Ashley's flesh and blood. How can you be so cruel?"

"Listen Laurent, or Larry; or whatever the hell she called you. She would never admit it, but I know you raped her and turned her into a whore. If she had testified like I wanted her to, you'd still be locked up like the animal you are."

"You ignorant bitch. If you hadn't destroyed my letters, things would have worked out differently."

"Sure they would. She'd be married to a damned mechanic. She was so worthy of much more than that. And if you call me a bitch again the cops will be there in a flash!"

"What the hell did you call for? You can't hurt Ashley any more and you sure as hell aren't going to get the chance to harm Ashleigh, either."

"Wouldn't waste my time. I called to make sure she was there. Now I don't have to report her as a runaway and I don't have to see her ever again."

He was not sure what it was, but when on the listening end and the phone is slammed back into its cradle, one knows the hang-up was not a gentle one.

Penny looked at me and asked, "Was that who I think it was?"

"My gramma?" Ashleigh asked.

Larry nodded. "Don't worry about it."

"Is she gonna try to make me go home?"

"No. You *are* at home, right here. In fact, she's glad you're OK."

"I'll bet. We have to go get my things."

"To your gramma's?"

Ashleigh smiled a little. "To the bus station. About a month ago, my mom and me took a couple small suitcases with my favorite stuff and put them in a locker."

She fished a key out of her sweater pocket and held it up. Larry took it from her and smiled.

"You seem to have planned this pretty carefully, like a prison break."

"It's funny you said that. Mom called it an escape."

"From what I heard from your grandmother, that's just what it was. Let's go. We can complete the mission together."

She gulped down the last of her milk and they started for the door.

"Can I come?" Moru asked.

"Sure," Ashleigh said. "C'mon."

At that moment, Larry saw that sure-fire confidence that was her mother's trait in her childhood. She had the same bold demeanor and he didn't know why, but he instantly thought that Ashleigh might do quite well in a spitting contest.

Penny was beaming. "I'll whip up a dessert for when you get back."

They retrieved her belongings, two small suitcases, from the bus station locker. On the way home, Moru and Ashleigh engaged in small talk about school, hobbies, favorite games and the like. Although a participant in the conversation, Ashleigh's responses were short, in monotones, but friendly. Larry was sure her feelings were conflicted and it would take some time before her true personality surfaced.

When they got back home, Penny prepared some sliced pound cake with ice cream for Moru and Ashleigh. Moru devoured; Ashleigh nibbled. Watching Ashleigh, Larry could see that she was exhausted. Even as she ate, her eyelids seem to get too heavy to support.

Penny noticed it quickly and ushered her off to the bedroom. *Oh-oh. That's our bedroom.* She returned in a matter of minutes and said, "She's pooped, but wants to talk to you."

"OK," Larry said, "but where are we going to sleep?"

"The couch pulls out, remember? And it's never been used."

He got up from the couch and went into Ashleigh's room. At least, it was Ashleigh's room for now, until they could fix up the den, game room, whatever. When he approached the bed, the light from a single bedside lamp shone gently on a picture of Ashley and it seemed that the light gently caressed her image, rather than shone upon it.

"She was beautiful," Ashleigh said.

"And so are you," Larry responded.

"I don't think I'll ever be that pretty," she said somberly.

She turned from the picture and looked at me. Tears were running down her cheeks. "Why was my gramma so mean to us?"

"I don't know, honey, but you don't have to worry about that ever again."

She sobbed. "She always loved you, y'know?"

"Your gramma?" Larry joked.

She managed a little smile that shone through the tears. "No. Mom."

"Oh. I thought that had a very unhappy ending for both of us, but I didn't know about you then. You're the happy ending we were cheated out of."

The tears were flowing more freely now. He handed her a tissue from the box on the nightstand.

"Did you really, really love her?"

"Oh, yes," he replied. "At the time, there was no one for me but my Ashley. However, it was she who decided that there was no magic left. She just wrote me a letter and went away."

She pounded her fist into the mattress and shouted, "God damn it, I miss her!"

Larry held her close and did his best to soothe her. He wanted to say something about her language, but her hurt was more important now and he simply held her until she cried herself out. Finally, she laid back and fell almost instantly to sleep.

Larry went back out to the living room and saw that the couch was now a bed, all made up and ready for a good night's sleep.

Penny looked up at me sheepishly and said, "I suppose you want to talk."

"You've got that right," he responded.

Chapter 12

It was a long night . . . they spent much of it talking.

"So, how long have you known about my daughter?" The phrase *my daughter* had a strange ring to it and Larry wondered how long it would take him to feel comfortable with that.

"It was about six months ago," Penny began. "Ashley called me and we met the next day. She told me then about the leukemia and although I felt sorry for her, I didn't know just then, why she was sharing that with me. Then she told me about Ashleigh and if it were possible, as the saying goes, my chin hit the floor. And a funny thing; all I could think about was you. You know, your sperm *wasn't* all that lazy. Those VA doctors jumped to a conclusion and we just bought into it. I felt like crap when I realized that."

"To hell with that," Larry said. "Why didn't you tell me? When did you decide that the kid would come here?"

"Don't call her *the kid.* She's your daughter. As your daughter, she's entitled to share a father's love, especially when the mother is gone. From what Ashley told me, her mother, the grandmother, would not have provided a home with much love in it. She sounded like a bitter old hag."

"Ashley or her mother?"

"Don't be flip. You know I meant her mother. When I met little Ashleigh, my heart went out to her. She was fully aware of what was happening and she asked a ton of questions about you."

"Like what?"

"Funny thing. She asked if you were better looking than she is."

"That's an odd question. What did you answer?" he asked.

"Well, I got a hunch that she wasn't pleased with her own looks in comparison to her mom's. I told her you were passable and not to worry. Look how well her mom turned out."

"Passable? Just passable?"

"Well, I didn't want her to think you were a Greek god or anything. I didn't want her to worry about unimportant things. So, I assured her you were a lovable, loving, gentle man who would love her just as much as her mom did."

"Hmmm. That sounds acceptable."

"Glad you like it. But I was torn over this. I really wanted to tell you, but Ashley was so afraid that you would force a meeting and with her prognosis, she didn't want any part of that. She thought it would put too much stress on Ashleigh."

"Damn. We better start calling her Ash. Ashley and Ashleigh sound the same."

"Yeah. That's what her mother called her."

"I suppose you have things all planned out?"

"Pretty much. I've contacted the school and they're expecting her whenever I call. I'll take her by there in the morning."

"I can't remember ever feeling so left out of something. To think that I have a daughter her age and never knew anything about it. Then my wife and my ex-girlfriend get together and hatch a plot like this."

"Oh, come on. We didn't hatch a plot. We just wanted to do what was best for Ash."

"Do you realize what feelings have been rekindled here? The way I felt about Ashley? Don't you feel threatened by that?"

"Why should I feel threatened?" Penny asked.

"Damn it, that kid is practically a clone of the Ashley I knew growing up. When I saw her standing in the doorway, I nearly flipped out. My God! The resemblance is staggering!"

"Well, I didn't know that. She didn't look anything like the Ashley I knew and I wondered where that straw-like hair came from; and the crooked teeth. The freckles I understood because Ashley still had those."

"I can't believe we're talking about such things. We now have a daughter. Moru has a sister. We are now a family of four; overnight."

"Yeah. And we need another bedroom."

"Hope we can afford it."

"Ashley wasn't wealthy, but she did OK. She set aside some for Ash, to help with her resettling."

"Good grief! Didn't you two overlook anything?"

"Don't think so," Penny said. "We also knew that if we did, you would come to the rescue."

She rolled close to him and kissed him lightly on the cheek.

"There you go with those feminine wiles again."

"Well, now that we know you don't have lazy sperm, shouldn't we give them some exercise?"

"Sometimes you can be downright evil," he said.

"Part of my charm."

"Shouldn't we sleep first?"

"Not a chance," she said. "I'm sad about Ashley, but really happy about our situation."

He rolled over on top of her. "This situation?"

"Now who's the evil one?" she giggled.

The next morning, Penny got up early and busied herself getting breakfast. She had already set the table for three when she realized that they were now four. As she was setting the fourth place, she heard Ashleigh stirring about her room. She approached the door, but stopped before opening it when she heard the sobbing. She paused for a moment, then knocked lightly and entered.

"Are you OK, Ash?"

"No," she whimpered.

"What's wrong?" As soon as Penny had asked, she realized what a stupid question that was. Then Ash responded in a way that inferred that she too, knew it was a stupid question.

"I just woke up in a strange bed because my mom's dead and I have a new home. I also have a father and a brother I never knew. What's wrong? I'm pissed off, that's what's wrong."

Penny approached her and held her close.

"I know, honey," Penny said. "It was a pretty stupid question, huh?"

"I'm not pissed off at the question or you. It's just . . ." Ashleigh never finished her answer as she broke down again and began to sob heavily.

Penny stood and took Ashleigh's hands in hers, saying, "Cry yourself out, honey . . . but if you're interested, I'm fixing breakfast."

With tears still streaming down her cheeks, Ashleigh forced a little smile and nodded. Penny left her and went back to the kitchen.

Ashleigh had made herself presentable before coming into the kitchen. Larry, Moru and Penny had just seated themselves. They all looked at Ashleigh and greeted her with smiles. Larry was once again amazed at the likeness of Ashleigh to the young girl Ashley with whom he had fallen in love. As he studied her, he recalled how his own Ashley had been transformed by braces and a hairdo and how well that could work again. *In due time,* he told himself.

"Do I have to start school right away?" Ash asked.

"Well, you don't want to miss too much," Larry said.

"I already had all her subjects," Moru quickly responded. "I can catch her up."

"A day or two wouldn't hurt," Penny said.

Ash was now enjoying her breakfast. Moru and Larry couldn't seem to keep their eyes off her. Penny noticed and remarked, "You two finish your breakfast and get out of here. Ash and I will spend a day or two getting acquainted."

"Don't you have to work at the hospital?" Larry asked.

"I'm just going in to arrange a day or two off. Ash can stay with me and then we girls are going shopping. I'm sure you need some things, right, Ash?"

"I guess," Ashleigh answered. Then she smiled a weak smile. "I'll know what I need when I see it."

"Spoken like a true shopper, and that's the scary part," Larry said.

Ashleigh's smile became more genuine as she looked at him. "Are you gonna like being my father?"

"No doubt about it."

Moru sat silently and noted that the others had all broken into smiles . . . he followed suit. He wasn't sure what having a sister was going to mean, but he had no fear that she would pose any threat to the relationship he enjoyed with Larry and Penny.

"Are you gonna like being my daughter?" Larry added.

Ash studied him for a moment, then looked toward Penny. She shrugged.

"You should probably ask that after she's been here a while," Penny said.

"I like you being here already," Moru said to Ash.

"Thanks," Ashleigh said with a smile.

"It's gonna sound real strange when I say 'my sister'," Moru said looking at her.

"I never said 'my brother' either," Ash responded. "We'll get used to it."

"I hope. It's gonna be nice with a sister to pick on."

"Don't get your hopes up," Ash responded quickly. "I may be little and a girl, but I'll still kick your ass."

"Just a minute, there," Larry interjected. "We have to have a long talk about your language, young lady. I'm sure your mom wouldn't have liked it either."

"Oh. I forgot to say *sorry for that.* Mom said that every time she cussed."

"It's not very ladylike to curse," Penny said gently.

"Yeah . . . I just slipped. Mom and I cussed only when we were alone. She told me that she and you," she said looking at Larry, "used to be able to cuss together real good."

Larry colored slightly, saying, "We were young and foolish back then."

"Yeah, I know. That's what I am now, but it will be easy to stop cussin' around you. I might have trouble finding words that mean the same . . . feel the same."

Larry smiled. "We can work on it together."

"I can help," Moru said.

"Don't you cuss outside?" Ash asked him.

Moru just looked at her as an awkward silence followed.

Ashley grinned broadly, saying, "Thought so."

"The dictionary is full of descriptive words, so when you feel like cussing, just go look up a word that isn't cussing, but expresses the same feeling," Moru said.

"Damn. Sounds like a homework assignment," Ash said. A silence followed then, with a half smirk she said, "Sorry for that."

They all smiled at that, but agreed that language improvement was to be a family goal.

Moru went off to school and Larry went off to work. Penny and Ashleigh just sat and looked at each other for a moment.

"Want some help with the cleanup?" Ash asked. "I always helped my mom, but it was usually just the two of us."

"You'll have to adjust to the heavy workload," Penny said with a grin.

"I guess. Let's get to it and go shopping. The first thing I want is my own clock radio. Mom had one that was real neat, but I think gramma took it. She came over one day and just helped herself to stuff. I didn't know what to do."

"Well, I'll never understand how your own grandmother could be so mean. But the first thing you and I have to do is to put your money into a bank account for you."

"I guess. Is eleven thousand dollars as much money as I think it is?"

"It's enough to buy a house if you had to. But we have to set up a plan so that you don't use up all the money before you need it to go to college."

"Mom never finished college, you know; even though she told everyone she did."

"Really? I didn't know that."

"It was my fault. I kinda broke up her senior year. Wasn't part of anyone's plan. That's when my gramma almost went nuts. From that day on, mom was *her whore* and I was *the little bastard*. After a while, it didn't even hurt when she said those things. Mom said that it showed how small her mind was. Some folks got that way from the war, I think."

"Well, you can forget the word *bastard* now that you're here. You're *our daughter*. I know that bastard isn't technically a swear word, but we should all put it to sleep; leave it completely out of our vocabulary."

Ashleigh's eyes gleamed with moisture and she smiled.

Penny looked at her a moment then said, "You may not think so now, but you are every bit as pretty as your mom was. Like she did, we can do a few simple things to really perk you up."

"Braces?"

"Later, maybe, but today, I think we can start with the hair. Why don't you get your mom's picture and bring it along. Maybe we can get a hairdresser who can do the same for you."

"The same color? And short? Like just over the ears?"

"Why not? You interested?"

"Oh, yes," Ashleigh beamed. "When can we go?"

"How about as soon as we finish here?"

It had been a long time since Ashleigh felt this level of happiness. Her excitement shone from her eyes and she seemed to be incapable of suppressing the smile that bisected her small face. They hurriedly dressed and went out the door. *The Hunt;* the shopping trip was launched.

Chapter 13

Both Moru and Larry were stunned at the vision that greeted them when they returned home. Ashleigh stood in the living room, neatly coiffed with short, auburn-colored hair. She wore stylish jeans and a beaded, sleeveless and V-necked tee shirt. They stood, silently looking her over.

"Well, dammit; *sorry for that.* Whatcha think?" With that, she spun around so that they could see all of her.

"Very impressive," Larry said. He could feel his throat tightening as he recalled the vision of his own Ashley when she first appeared with her own new hairdo.

"Sexy, too," Moru added. "Ooops. *Sorry for that.* I can't wait to show you off at school, and you know I'm gonna have to fight the boys off for you."

"No need. I can kick . . . butt if I have to."

"Nice catch," Moru said with a smile.

"Yeah," Ash said as she lowered her eyes. "*Almost* sorry for that."

Penny was beaming. "I also made an appointment with an orthodontist."

Larry felt a lump rising in his throat as his mind wandered back to the first time he saw, and kissed Ashley, with her new braces. He felt the moistness in his eyes and the reincarnated vision of his Ashley blurred. He said nothing. He approached Ash and broke into an approving smile. He held her close, then whispered, "You're going to be even prettier than your mom."

She looked up at him and smiled. Her eyes, too, showed signs of tearing.

"I hope so," she said, then excused herself and went to her room. Larry suspected she was probably going to cry. He felt that he could easily do that, too.

"They call that a transformation," Moru said. "What a difference that color makes."

"Wait 'til you see her after the braces do their work," Penny said.

Moru left the room. Penny and Larry sat there just looking at each other. Neither spoke. It seemed they each recognized Larry's need to compose himself to make sure his voice would work without tremor.

Finally, Larry posed an interesting question. "What's your purpose in making Ash over to look like her mother?"

"What?"

"What you're doing is recreating the young Ashley I was in love with. I got over that when I married you, but now it all comes rushing back. It's downright eerie."

"Have you considered that it's my effort to make this discovery; this emergence of an unknown child, as pleasant as possible for you?"

"I haven't considered anything. Everything's so damned new and Ash has stirred memories long buried. I guess I'm still confused, surprised; no, shocked."

"If anything I'm doing causes you pain, let me know. That's the last thing I want to do. I thought you would just experience warm fuzzy thoughts. You know, the fondest memories."

"But don't you see some conflict there? I mean, Ashley was my first love and you're resurrecting her memory. You should feel threatened by that, I would think."

"Nonsense. Ashley's gone; she's part of your past. And that past produced a beautiful little girl who is part of your present. It's not what I'm doing that's arousing those old feelings, it's Ash. If your behavior looks threatening to me, you'll be the first to know. Now, I'd rather stop discussing this and just go about being a family."

"It will take some adjustment, huh?"

It was an easier adjustment than Larry expected. They all settled into a family routine that seemed to glide effortlessly through family squabbles, tensions over homework and the like. Any casual observer would have to conclude that here was a happy family; and they would have been right to do so.

Moru excelled in both sports and academics and during his high school years and it soon became evident that he was destined to a college education on a baseball scholarship. Ash, two years behind Moru, was an average student, but found her area of excellence in the study of drama and theatre. During Moru's senior high school year, the first major problem arose, leading to a family crisis that Larry and Penny had never thought possible.

Ash and Moru were as close as any natural siblings ever were and therein lay the problem. They were attracted to each other . . . in love not as siblings, but as boyfriend and girlfriend. They went out to eat together. They went to the movies together. Neither was seeing other boys or girls. They were "steadies" as surely as Larry and Ashley had been at their age. As might be expected, they had achieved a level in their relationship that was to lead to sexual discovery. They had suppressed their urges for as long as they could. As it had happened many years before, Ash initiated the inevitable.

"When you kiss me goodnight," she said to Moru, "I feel like you're doing more than just a goodnight kiss."

Moru flushed. "What do you mean?"

"Sometimes I think you'd like to kiss me at other times, too."

Moru looked at her and responded only with a weak smile.

"Like now. Wouldn't you like to kiss me now?"

Moru looked down at his hands, wondering what best to do with them.

Ash leaned toward him and offered her mouth to him. Moru was blushing now as he tried to figure how to handle this situation. Then, Ash handled it for him. She placed her mouth on his and licked his lips. As if she had pulled a trigger, Moru responded and they locked in a tight embrace and enjoyed a long, passionate kiss.

"That was really good, huh?" Ashley asked, catching her breath.

"I wondered how good it would be. I've wanted to kiss you like that for a long time."

"We're lucky I don't have a boyfriend and you don't have a girlfriend. Now we can be a couple."

"What? Are you nuts? We're brother and sister. We can't do that." Moru blurted, but even as he said it, he wished it wasn't so.

"We're only related on paper. That brother and sister stuff is if you have the same parents and we don't, so there." She wrapped her arms around him again and kissed him passionately. Moru quickly reciprocated, feeling too weak to resist.

The passionate kissing led to fondling and finally, Ash said, "If we're going to do anything else, we have to get protection."

Moru looked at her. "You're kidding, right?"

"No. I'm ready for sex and I don't want to do it with anyone but you," she whispered. "Can you handle that?"

Moru turned away and took a few steps before turning to face her. "I don't know if I can handle it, but I really want you now. Physically. Well, you know how boys are. But it's wrong, Ash. What would mom and dad think?"

"I didn't plan on telling them."

"Oh, my God. That just makes it seem even more wrong."

"What do you think? Like we should go tell mom and dad that we want to shack up?"

"Hell, no. But they're sure to find out."

"Not if we're careful. You know, discreet."

"Listen to us. We're talking like we are already in favor of doing it."

"Well, I am. Aren't you?"

Ash walked over to Moru and kissed him again. Fondling followed and they soon forgot the caveat about protection. Perhaps it was the "forbidden sex" attitude about their actions, but the sex was intense and satisfying.

"Wow," Ash sighed. "That was wonderful. It was everything they said in the books I read."

"Books?"

"Oh, those cheap romance novels. They describe sex like it's always the best ever."

"How could it be the best ever? It was our first."

"Yup. And all the rest will be measured against how good it was this time."

Moru didn't respond. With the release of sexual tension came new concerns about what they had just done. The thought of continuing a sexual relationship with his stepsister didn't sound at all like a reasonable pursuit. Those thoughts were quickly dispelled as Ash rolled atop him and began kissing him once again.

Over the next couple of months, they enjoyed each other sexually whenever they could be alone. They were discreet and careful and soon, they realized they were very much in love.

One evening, as they sat around the table after dinner, Penny said, "I'm beginning to wonder about you two. Kids your age are all about dating and mixing with your friends. You two seem to stay pretty isolated from all that."

Moru felt an inner panic rising from the pit of his stomach. He said nothing, but he felt flushed.

"Oh, look," Ash said. "You've made Moru blush. He's embarrassed."

Larry chuckled. "Nothing to be embarrassed about, son. Urges toward the opposite sex are completely natural at your age. I just hope you'll come to us to discuss any of your concerns."

"So, do you have a girl friend we don't know about, Moru?" Ash asked.

Penny smiled and said, "Don't embarrass him any further, Ash. He'll surface when he's ready."

"Well," Ash said, "I don't have enough time to waste on boys. I don't mind if they kiss me as part of a play we're in, but with braces, I'm inclined to wait."

"Have any of them made any advances?" Larry asked.

"You'll know when that happens," Ash said with a grin. "He'll be the one with the black eye."

They laughed. Moru was relieved that Ash had diverted the conversation away from him.

Larry remembered how Ashley had bloodied Bobby's nose and couldn't suppress a smile. "I pity the poor jerk," he said.

They laughed again and the question of dating went no further.

After the table had been cleared, Moru and Ash spread out their homework in front of them, while Larry and Penny adjourned to the living room to watch television.

"That was scary," Moru muttered quietly. "I almost blew it. Thanks for stepping in and saving me."

"Saving *us*," Ash responded. "If they thought for a minute about what we're doing, your blushing would have been like a confession."

"I couldn't help it. I thought my head was going to pop. Sweat even ran down my rib cage. Near panic."

"I guess I got it from my mom, but I'm pretty fast on my feet when I need to be."

"I'll say. When you started talking about giving some jerk a black eye, I couldn't believe what happened."

"What do you mean, what happened?"

"I got hot; you know. Man, you were at your sexiest. So calm. So cool."

"You mean you wanted me?"

"Yup. Still do."

"You're an animal," she said, grinning.

"Yup. I guess I am when it comes to you."

"Do your homework."

"Yeah. You, too."

After a while, Ash looked up and said, "You know they'll find out sooner or later."

"How? We've been pretty careful."

"I just feel it. How are we going to handle that?"

Moru didn't respond due to the entrance of Penny. "You kids still at it?"

"We're done," Ash said. "Just talking about what kind of person we would date if we started that stuff."

Moru felt that familiar feeling as he flushed. Ash grinned at his discomfort. He glowered at her.

"Oh, Ash; look what you've done. Poor Moru is blushing again."

"Cut it out you two. I can't help it."

"I bet when you get a girl and really kiss her the first time, you'll have to go change your underwear," Ash said with a giggle.

"Ashleigh!" Penny shouted. "That was totally crude!"

"OK; *sorry for that,*" Ash responded.

Moru got up from the table, gathered his books together and left the room.

Penny looked at Ash and broke into a smile. "We were pretty rough on him."

"He can handle it," Ash said. "I just hope he isn't, you know, into boys."

"How can you even think such a thing?" Penny looked shocked.

Ash just shrugged. She gathered up her homework, feeling that the seed she had just planted would put sex between her and Moru the farthest thing from her parents' minds.

Chapter 14

Moru and Ash successfully continued their assignations, avoiding both detection and pregnancy. In their good luck, they were ecstatically happy with each other. As Moru's graduation approached and his departure for college neared, Ash was becoming frantic. She wondered how she would be able to handle the weeklong separations while he was away. On weekends when he had ball games, she would face more and more periods of loneliness. Although not discussed, it became a tension between them that intensified their sexual encounters.

"Lately, every time seems better than the last," Ash said as they lay together.

"I know," Moru said. "I think it's because I'll be going away.'

She pounded her fist on his chest. "Don't mention that!"

"Ow," he said. "But it's only a month away."

She pounded his chest again.

"Stop that! One more time and I'll have to punish you."

She did it again. He pulled her close and rolled atop her. "Please try not to scream."

Their union was complete and satisfying.

"I need a shower," Ash said as she tumbled out of bed and got to her feet.

"What a great body you have," Moru said admiringly.

"Animal."

She walked to the door and opened it. Penny was standing there, poised to knock on the door. Ash jumped with a start. Moru pulled the bed sheet over his head.

"Oh, my God!" Penny shouted. "What are you two doing?"

After a pause of only a few seconds, seconds that seemed to drag on into minutes, Ash turned toward Moru and couldn't help but laugh at the vision of Moru with the sheet pulled over his head. In his haste to cover his face, he had exposed his lower body.

"What would you prefer me to say?" Ash asked, red-faced. "Nothing? Just fooling around? Having sex?"

Penny was aghast. She could feel the anger throughout her body. Her throat tightened; her teeth were so tightly clenched her jaw hurt; she felt a trembling sensation in her stomach.

"You two get dressed and get yourselves downstairs. Moru, for God's sake, pull the sheet down and cover yourself. You have just made a total sham of this family. You can bet there will be hell to pay for this."

Penny whirled around and went downstairs, obviously in great distress.

"Oh, shit," Moru said as he got out of the bed. "We've got real trouble now."

"I still need a shower. You can get dressed and go downstairs and wait for me, if you want to."

"Are you kidding? She's mad enough to castrate me if she can get me alone."

"Oh, don't let her do that. We may want to have children some day." She smiled.

"Are you nuts? They'll probably send you off to a convent and me to a monastery."

"I, unlike you, have considered this possibility and have it all figured out, so don't worry. They'll get over it."

She went into the bathroom to take her shower. Moru stood there, then began to dress himself. Normally, he would have showered with Ash, but that didn't seem like an appropriate course of action now.

What the hell was Penny doing home so early? There were three hours left on her shift at the hospital and Larry wasn't due for another hour beyond that.

Penny bellowed from the downstairs living room. "Hurry up, damn you!" There was a catch in her curse and Moru realized that she was starting to cry. Maybe they could handle that emotion more easily than her rage.

When Ash and Moru went downstairs, they found Penny crying. Moru thought then that maybe her rage would have been better. He and Ash felt sorry for obviously hurting Penny, but didn't regret their love for each other. They both realized the severity of the problem. Moru was extremely anxious, but Ash seemed to remain composed, ready to confront the problem.

Penny used a tissue to dry her eyes and clear her nose and looked up at them. Drying her eyes hadn't helped. New tears ran down her cheeks.

"I have never been so profoundly shocked about anything in my entire life!"

"We're in love," Ash said.

"You don't even know the meaning of the word!" Penny shouted.

"Yes, we do," Moru said quietly. "It's all around us."

"Yes," Ash said. "You and dad have showered us with so much caring and love, it was natural for us to love one another."

"Sibling love *does not* include sex!" Penny continued shouting. "That's incest!"

"How so?" Ash asked defiantly. "We're only related on paper. For God's sake, he isn't even of the same race, but that didn't stop my attraction to him."

"Don't you use that warped teen-age logic on me, young lady. I called your father. I expect him to be here soon. You two have broken our hearts."

"I thought you would be happy that Moru and I could find such a deep love so early in our lives."

"What? Happy? Are you delusional? Don't you even realize what you have done?"

"We just fell in love," Moru tried to be part of the exchange. Unfortunately, he wasn't as prepared as Ash always seemed to be when it came to arguing a point.

"Stop that!" Penny shouted again. "*You're not in love!* You can't be in love! Not that kind of love. You're brother and sister!"

"Look," Ash said. "If anything, we're only adopted relatives. There's no blood connection here and that's what the law is all about. We're just two teenagers who have found each other. That's better than screwing around with all of our high school buddies like the other kids are doing."

"Watch your language, young lady."

"It's true," Moru said. "All my friends are having sex with girls at school."

"And you think that makes what you're doing right?"

"It's better than what the others are doing," Ash said. "Everybody is having sex. At least with me and Moru it has meaning beyond the physical pleasure."

"My God," Penny looked stunned. "What have you been reading? It sounds like you've been researching the topic."

"I have. I didn't want to be called a whore like my gramma called my mom. I wanted our sex to mean something and I never did it with anyone else, because I was sure I wanted Moru to be my first and only."

"I can't believe this. What has happened to you two?"

"We grew up," Ash said. "If we hadn't had each other, who knows what we might have done? At least, we only did it at home and with each other."

"And that's supposed to warrant my thanks?" Penny was astounded. "Oh, how lucky we are!" she said mockingly. "Our kids only have sex at home and with each other!"

"Mom," Moru said, "we didn't want to hurt you. We didn't want to hurt anyone. Our first time was almost an accident, then we realized that it was meant to be."

"Which one of you was the aggressor? There had to be a first move."

Without hesitation, Ash said, "I started it. I felt Moru and I belonged together and soon after we started, so did he. It's been blissful."

"You've been reading those sick romance novels, haven't you?"

"They're your books, not mine," Ash said.

"That's enough of your smart-aleck talk. Go to you room until your father comes home. And Moru, you stay down here. No way I'm letting you two alone up there."

"Are you going to put bars on our doors?" Ash asked, now assuming an angrier tone.

"Enough smart talk. Move it!" Penny said pointing the way upstairs.

Ash hurried up the stairs while Moru continued to stand awkwardly where he had stood during the entire exchange.

"Sit!" Penny commanded.

Moru sat, his mind awhirl with questions. *What would dad think? What kind of punishment would they impose? What will happen between him and Ash? Would this destroy or reinforce their love for each other?*

When he came home, Larry went into the kitchen with Penny. They closed the door behind them. As Moru sat there, he could hear their voices rise from time to time but was unable to understand all that was being said. It took Penny longer than Moru thought necessary to report that he and Ash were caught in a sexual situation. Each time the conversation paused, he expected Larry to come charging out of the room to beat him senseless. He didn't know why he thought that, because Larry had not struck him since his early "rascally" years and then he had resorted only to light bottom spanking.

Larry soon came out of the kitchen and stood silent, glowering at Moru. "What the hell were you thinking?"

Moru sat silent and merely shrugged.

"I can't think of anything in my whole life that I find as disgusting and disappointing as this. Having sex with your sister is sick; it's incest!"

Moru responded almost instantly. "No, it isn't. We aren't even related except on those scraps of paper you have. We started out as loving siblings, then the rest just happened. We couldn't control it."

"*Couldn't?* Don't you mean *wouldn't?*"

"We just started with the sex. We were going to stop, but we fell in love with each other. We even hope to get married someday."

"Just listen to yourself! How in heaven's name do you hope to marry? Papers or not, she's legally your step-sister and I'm sure the courts are very set on that sort of thing."

"Set on what? Two young people, unrelated, fall in love. So what's the big deal?"

Larry looked perplexed. "How long have you two been having sex together?"

"Couple, three months," Moru lied.

"My God, Moru! What if you had gotten her pregnant?"

"Well, Ash says she'd like to have a kid together some day. Then we could probably be married without any of the legal bullshit."

"Watch your tongue. That's out of the question. I can't believe you would do this to us. Penny and I have been as good a set of parents you could have hoped for and this is how you repay us."

"This isn't about you, dad. It's about Ash and me, and fate. After all, you brought us together."

"So what does that make me, your pimp? Your poor mother is a basket case in there," Larry said pointing to the closed kitchen door.

"He didn't mean it that way," Ash said as she came down the stairs. "And he's right; it's about us, not you."

Moru stood as Ash approached them. He extended his hand and she took it. Then she raised their clasped hands and said to Larry, "See this? Our hands are bonding us together. We have become one, just like it says in the bible. If we have to leave here in order to fulfill our destiny, then so be it."

With that, she led Moru to the doorway, preparing to exit the house.

"Don't you dare leave like this."

"Oh, we'll be back. As soon as you and Penny sort this thing out so that we can all concentrate on happiness instead of this stupid conflict."

They left the house together. At the sound of the door closing, Penny came out of the kitchen, all teary-eyed.

"Where are they going? Why did you let them go?" she shouted at Larry.

"Well I wasn't going to act like a linebacker and tackle them. They left so we could talk this out, I guess."

"Talk? Good grief; I don't want to talk. I feel like hitting something . . . hard."

"We have a lot to think about. Somehow, we have to dissuade them from this stupid course of action."

When Ash and Moru left the house, they walked hurriedly, hand in hand, with no specific destination in mind.

"I figured we'd get caught sooner or later," Ash said, speaking at a rapid rate equal to their walking pace. "We got a little too comfortable with it. Now we have to convince them how right this is."

"Yeah, but we can't just start right in with the sex again. We really hurt them. Maybe we're gonna have to cool it," Moru said.

"We just don't do it at home, that's all. We can do it wherever we're alone."

"Boy, I don't know. If we get caught again, there really would be hell to pay."

"So, we don't get caught. It's that simple. C'mon, the park's just around the corner. I'll show you how easy it is and how really good it can be."

"How can you even think about that now?"

"Because getting caught got me all excited." She turned into him and planted a passionate kiss on him. It didn't take much coaxing until Moru responded. They had entered the park and settled on a bench where they continued to arouse each other.

They were oblivious to the approach of two young men. They caroused the park, looking for something to do. In Ash, they found their something. Before they realized what was happening, Moru was struck from behind, knocked to the ground, where one of the men started kicking him around the chest and head. The other man engaged Ash, expecting little resistance. He slapped her twice when she lashed out with her foot and caught him in the groin. She kicked him again along side his jaw, snapping his head around. Moru was now out of it, so the other man grabbed Ash from behind and started delivering a series of kidney punches. The other man, regaining some of his composure approached and began delivering punishing blows to Ash's face.

Ash could feel the impact of the blows, but the pain was yet to surface. She felt the bone in her nose crack and she knew that blood was flowing freely.

The man stopped hitting her and said, "Now you're gonna pay for resisting you little bitch!"

She wanted to answer him; curse him; but she was unable to speak. She was aware that her clothes were being torn from her body. She was suddenly thrown to the ground and raped. Every time she tried to resist, another blow came into her ribs, her face, until she lapsed into unconsciousness. Fortunately, she was not aware of the continuing rapes and the unspeakable acts that followed.

They laughed and left her for dead.

Chapter 15

Moru and Ash had laid on the ground in the park for nearly an hour before some passers by noticed them and called police. Moru was badly beaten but all of his injuries were survivable. Ashley, however, was near death. The EMTs worked feverishly over her, hooking up IVs, assisting her breathing and monitoring her vital signs. Her beaten and bloodied body was rushed to the hospital. Moru, in an adjacent stretcher, merely moaned in pain and discomfort.

"Ash, Ash." He called her name repeatedly, but was unable to say anything else. Their conditions were closely monitored as the ambulance raced toward the hospital, red lights and siren warning all other motorists to clear the way. Close behind, a police car followed in full emergency mode.

At the hospital, nurses and police tried to determine their identities, but the assailants had taken all their possessions, including identification. Moru was quickly treated for some fractured ribs, a cracked breastbone and broken collarbone. When it was determined he could be moved, he was sent to the ICU for continued monitoring. On his chart was entered the name, John Doe.

In the ER, meanwhile, doctors and nurses worked feverishly on Jane Doe: Ash. In very short order, she was whisked away to an operating room for some *major repair work,* as the surgeon had described it.

While in surgery, a patrolman reported finding their wallets. The

Does were now properly identified and Larry and Penny were called with the grim news.

They arrived at the hospital in a state of near panic. They were taken to Moru's room, where Penny broke down at the sight of him. Larry had to hold her as he led her to the chair beside Moru's bed.

"My God," Larry muttered. "What have they done to him?"

A nurse entered the room. "Mr. St. Jacques? There was a young lady name Ashleigh Cummings with your son. She's badly hurt and is in surgery. Do you know her?"

"She's my daughter," Larry said. "It's a long story," he added after a pause.

"Better come with me," the nurse said.

"Go," Penny sobbed. "I'll stay with Moru."

Larry followed the nurse to the surgery waiting room where he sat. In a matter of moments, a doctor entered.

"Mr. St. Jacques, I'm Doctor Carlisle, head of the surgery department. I'm afraid your daughter has been severely beaten and sexually assaulted. We may have to remove her spleen and her uterus. She's bleeding internally and will need some liver repair. We've ordered her specific blood type for transfusion and we're giving her some universal blood until it arrives."

"For God's sake, don't wait. I'll give her some of mine; as much as she needs."

"OK. I'll send in a phlebotomist to check out your blood."

"Hell, she's my daughter; what's to check out?"

"Routine procedure that we can't bypass, Mr. St. Jacques. It won't take long and we'll be able to transfuse well before the blood bank supply arrives."

In a matter of minutes, his blood had been drawn and rushed to the lab. He had trouble sitting still in the waiting room. He got up, paced about, sat back down, got up again, paced about some more. He waited for nearly 45 minutes and no one came to set up the transfusion. He was sure the blood bank's supply had arrived by now. Maybe these folks were just too slow to handle this kind of action.

He opened the door to the waiting room and stepped into the hall. Facing him were the doors to the surgical suite. He knew he couldn't go in there, but the urge to do so was very strong. Before he could act, the doors swung open and Dr, Carlisle approached him.

"It's done," Carlisle said. "She's a tough young lady. As I mentioned, we had to remove the spleen and the uterus, as well as a portion of her liver, which had a tear in it. The remaining portion of the liver pinked up nicely after surgery and we expect your daughter to have a full recovery. Unfortunately, she will need some facial reconstruction, but we have an excellent plastic surgeon here that will do a nice job."

"Good Lord, what did they do to her?"

"We can only guess, but it was brutal. We've had patients who had to be pried out of car wrecks who suffered fewer injuries than that. She also has a head trauma and we're checking that out now."

"When can I see her?"

"Well, that's the rest of the story, I'm afraid. She's in a coma right now, but that's not uncommon for what she's been through. It's nature's way of preventing further harm. She should be out of it in a few days or a week, but you can see her as soon as we get her settled in her room."

"What happened to the blood problem?"

"Oh, yes. It didn't match. We assume your daughter is adopted. I'd have to run more conclusive tests, but it seems there's no way you could be her biological father."

"What?"

"It was not a match, Mr. St. Jacques. Is there a problem?"

"Damn right there's a problem. That girl is my daughter. Her biological mother is dead, but at one time, we were very close. I didn't know about her until her mom died."

"Well, we can do further testing, if you wish."

"Yes, I wish. This is the most bizarre thing I've ever heard. Your lab had to make a mistake."

"We'll check it out for you."

"Damn straight, you will."

Larry stormed down the hall toward the elevator. He returned to Moru's room where Penny, more composed now, sat holding Moru's hand.

"How's Ash?" she anxiously asked.

"Serious, but the doctor thinks she'll be OK after some reconstructive surgery. They had to remove her spleen, part of her liver and her uterus."

"Oh, my God! She'll never have children! What did those animals do to her?"

"They're calling it sexual assault, plus multiple rapes and abuse."

Penny could hardly catch her breath. Before she could respond to that, there was a soft knock on the door. It opened and a detective and a uniformed officer entered the room.

"I hope you can spare us a few minutes. I'm detective Robinson and I'd like to ask a few questions."

"Of course," Larry sighed in resignation. "Fire away."

"You are the parents of the two victims?"

Larry didn't respond. The very question set his mind awhirl. *How the hell do I answer that one?*

After a pause, Penny answered, "Yes, we are."

She looked at Larry. "Are you all right?" she asked him.

"Yes, we are," he echoed. He looked at Penny. "I'll be fine."

"Do you know what they were doing in the park?"

Larry thought, *yes, having sex, probably*, but he said nothing.

"They just left the house together to go for a walk," Penny said.

"Did they do that often? I mean, was there a pattern someone may have spotted?"

"You mean they might have been stalked?" Larry asked.

"Possibly. They're not the first young couple accosted in that park."

"And what are the police doing about it?" Larry asked belligerently.

"Never had much to go on until tonight. Your kids' IDs had been removed from their wallets, so we're hoping for some fingerprints."

"How much do you want to let me at them first?" Larry asked.

"I didn't hear that," Robinson said.

"Yeah, I know. *Sorry for that.*" Larry was beginning to feel a vile, angry feeling rising from his stomach. "I just hope you have to beat the crap out of them taking them down."

Robinson smiled. "I know how you feel, Mr. St. Jacques, but I can't promise."

"Anything else?" Penny asked.

"Only if you think of something you haven't already told us. Especially if you learn that someone had something against your kids."

"Believe me," Larry said, "we'll call in a minute."

"Thank you. Try to get some rest. Tomorrow, our detective branch will be developing a series of questions trying to come up with some leads. We'll call you."

"Thanks," Penny said.

Larry merely nodded at Robinson.

After Robinson and the patrolman left the room, Larry fell heavily into a chair. "My whole Goddamn world is crashing down around me," he muttered.

"What?"

"That damned doctor upstairs told me that Ash is not my daughter. Can you believe that horseshit?"

"He told you what!"

"From our blood match, or rather no match, he said that it was unlikely that Ash was my daughter. They're running a couple more tests."

"Oh, my God. That can't be! Ashley told me you were Ash's father. She told Ash in that note and told her all about what you were to each other."

"Lies? Who knows. I'm praying it was some sort of mistake in the lab. We'll wait."

Wait they did. Penny arranged to stay at the hospital for one night, at least. Larry went home and returned with some clothes and toiletries for her and by the time he got home, it was past midnight. He was too disturbed to go to bed, so he slipped on a sweater and walked to the park. He saw a police car sitting near a park bench and as he approached, he could see the yellow crime scene tape around the bench and some thirty yards around it. He went up to the car and introduced himself.

The patrolman got out of the car and shook Larry's hand.

"I'm sorry for your troubles," he said. "Are they going to be alright?"

"My daughter's in a coma after major surgery. My son is beaten up but will be OK. They both have a long recovery ahead."

"I wish you all the best. You realize that I can't let you onto the scene?"

"Yes, I do," Larry said. "I couldn't sleep so just started walking. Didn't intend to come here, but here I am."

"I hope we get the scum who did this."

"Me too, officer."

He turned away, then said, "If you get to nab these guys, kick 'em in the balls for me."

The officer smiled, gave Larry a casual salute and said, "Goodnight."

Larry walked back home and went to bed.

The telephone rang with the intensity of a fire alarm as Larry sat upright in bed. He realized it was only the phone. He glanced at the bedside clock and noticed it was five o'clock in the morning.

He snatched the receiver and said, "Yes?"

"Moru's awake," Penny's voice came to him, further penetrating his sleep-foggy brain.

"I'll be right there," he said.

"Take your time. He's slipping in and out and he hasn't said anything yet. On your way over here, pick me up a cup of coffee from Harry's. This hospital stuff tastes burnt. I don't think they know how to make it fresh."

"OK. I'll be there in an hour or so. Love you."

"Of course you do," she said.

There was something in her tone that conveyed a sense that everything would be all right. He knew that one of Penny's strengths was optimism that seemed to make things come out just fine. *God, I hope she can "optimism" us out of this mess.*

Chapter 16

The next day, doctors confirmed that there was no way that Larry could be Ashleigh's biological father. He and Penny were stunned. They had been certain that the hospital had made a mistake.

"How are we going to tell her?" Larry wondered aloud.

"Tell her? Absolutely not. You can't tell her that after losing her mother, she's lost her father, too. This is something we should never, ever, tell her."

"But maybe she would like to find her real father."

"You *are* her real father. Forget biology. You're the only father she knows. She loves you. And we love her. We can just leave it at that."

"Remember that she and Moru were already thinking about marriage? It seems now that it could probably be legally arranged."

"Come on, Larry. They're children. They have no idea of what they want yet."

"You think it's just hormones? I saw the love in that girl's eyes whenever she looked at Moru. The only thing that floored me was that they were already having sex."

"Well that will have to stop. With the extent of Ash's injuries, we may not have to worry about it for a while. This coffee's great," she added as she sipped. "Thanks."

The door opened and a nurse entered. Moru was still sleeping.

"We have to do a few chores for Moru, if you don't mind. You can visit with your daughter now. She's still in a coma, but she's all cleaned up and presentable."

They left together and walked hurriedly toward the elevator. When they got to Ash's room, they entered and Penny froze in the doorway. It was her first look at Ashleigh and had no idea what to expect. What she saw aroused every fear a mother can experience at such a time.

Ash's head was bandaged. *They had mentioned head trauma casually. Probably because it wasn't as serious as the organ damage.* Tubes were inserted into her nose, another hung loosely from her lips; her lips, so battered, her mouth was one huge mass of swollen, bloody tissue. Penny wondered if her beautiful, straightened teeth had been damaged. She noticed the bags hanging on the side of the bed. Being a nurse, she immediately looked to see if there was any urine collecting. She felt relief when she noticed the evidence that her kidneys were still functioning.

Her hands were wrapped in bloodstained bandages and there were huge bruises on her arms. *Defensive wounds. Her Ash was a fighter.* Both eyes were swollen nearly shut and there was a deep cut, already stitched up, above her left eyebrow.

She and Larry stood by the bed, tightly gripping hands. Tears flowed down Penny's cheeks, and soon, she broke down and cried openly.

"Oh, God. What have they done to our little girl?" she spoke between sobs.

"If I ever get my hands on those bastards, I'll kill 'em."

Penny didn't answer. They continued to stand silently by Ash's bed. A nurse entered.

"May I view her chart?" Penny asked. "I'm a nurse."

She accepted the chart the nurse handed her and as Penny viewed it, a look of concern came over her face.

She looked at the nurse and asked, "Is the swelling because of bleeding in the brain?"

"I'm afraid so," answered the nurse. "The doctor will be in shortly to explain how we are going to relieve the pressure. She should be just fine after that."

Penny looked at Larry. They said nothing. Then they held each other.

Weeks passed and Ashleigh remained unconscious. The bleeding in her brain had been checked and the swelling had subsided. Doctors cautioned that there could be some minor brain damage, but that the brain was quite capable of self-healing and rerouting normal tasks within itself. This was little comfort to Larry and Penny who watched anxiously for any sign of a return to awareness.

Weeks later, Moru, though bruised and sore, was healing and almost back to normal. He was unable to play baseball, but his total recovery was expected soon. He was devastated about Ash's condition and felt the first pangs of a love lost. He blamed himself and knew that Ash was likely to do the same when she became aware of all that had happened to her.

Larry and Penny had made a solemn pact never to reveal that Ashleigh's biological father was once again unknown.

"She doesn't need to know this," Penny had insisted. "She's been through enough."

"We have to keep it from Moru, too," Larry had cautioned. "If he ever blurted that out, it would destroy her."

"It kind of puts their promiscuous behavior on a back burner, doesn't it?"

"God, I hate to think it, but maybe this was a reckoning."

"Larry; surely you don't believe that."

"I don't want to, but it's there in the back of my mind."

"I don't think it works that way. Have you heard anything from the police?"

"They're still waiting for results of the fingerprints on the kids' IDs. They've had some difficulty separating out Moru's and Ash's."

They sat at Ash's bedside, talking in hushed tones. What they had waited for so long finally happened. Ashleigh opened her eyes and started looking around. Penny was the first to notice the sudden awareness.

"Larry! Look! She's awake!"

She touched Ash's hand and forced a smile, saying, "Oh, honey, we were so worried. You were so badly beaten, we thought we had lost you."

Larry said nothing as he formed a silent prayer of thanks in his mind. With tear-filled eyes, he looked down at his daughter and tried to suppress his sobs. He failed.

Ash didn't speak. She looked at them with a questioning look.

Penny rushed to the door and summoned the ward nurse, who hurried to the bedside.

"Well, welcome to the wide awake world, young lady," the nurse said, smiling.

The nurse quickly checked her vital signs and smiled again. "I'll contact her doctor," the nurse said. "You have no idea how anxious he's been. He knew she would come out of the coma, but there was never any telling when."

She left the room and Larry and Penny returned to hovering over Ash's bed.

Ashleigh merely looked at them, then as if a light of recognition turned on somewhere in her brain, a slight smile played across her lips.

Larry and Penny were laughing and crying. It was impossible for them to separate the two emotions. They were also at a loss for words. They stroked Ash's hands, her arms; it seemed they had to have that sense of touch to assure that the moment was real.

The next morning, the doctor visited and prescribed a regimen that would wean her off the feeding tube and, eventually, return her bodily functions to normal. Throughout the entire day, however, Ashleigh said not a word. She merely looked around the hospital room and occasionally, her eyes rested on Larry or Penny and that slight smile would appear once again.

That evening, Moru came with his parents to see her. He was apprehensive, fearing that their first meeting after the incident would prove to be unpleasant. What happened *was* unpleasant, but not in the way Moru had feared. Ash merely looked at him and did not respond to his soft touch and kind words. She merely looked at him and no emotion registered. Then she would look to Larry or Penny with an expression that suggested the question, "Who's this?"

"She acts like she doesn't know me," Moru said, obviously hurt.

"There was some brain injury and bleeding," Larry told him. "She'll probably need some time for all her memories to come back. She can't talk yet. She just stares and every once in a while, it looks like she wants to smile."

Moru looked at Ash. She had lost weight. She was almost colorless. *Could this still be the girl I love? What if she dumps me after this? What's going to happen to us?*

"Remember what I told you, Moru," Penny began in a whisper, repeating what the doctors had told her, "she may not even remember the assault, so don't say anything to remind her. Whatever memories she may have lost will come back in time."

Moru wondered if she would remember their sexual bond. *What if she doesn't even remember* that*? I want my Ash back. What am I going to do without her?*

"She's going to be here for a while, then she'll have to face months of rehab, according to her doctor. You two are not going to be alone together for a long time, if ever," Larry admonished him.

"What do you think I am?' Moru asked, astonished that his father would think ill of him at a time like this. "I only want her to get well. I know how you two feel about our relationship, but we can cool it until she's well enough to decide what we want to do."

"What you *want* to do is irrelevant," Penny said. "What matters is what you're *going* to do, and that is nothing further. We adopted you and we can disown you just as easily if you ever molest your sister again."

"I didn't molest her," Moru said quietly but angrily. "It was mutual. We shared."

Penny clapped her hands over her ears.

"Enough," she hissed. "I'll hear no more about it. It's sick!"

Although Larry was in complete agreement, he couldn't help feeling empathy toward his young son who was suffering a loss, just as surely and he had with his own Ashley years ago. He placed his hand on Moru's shoulder. "Not here; not now," he said.

Moru nodded. Penny agreed.

"Da..." Ash tried to speak.

All three hovered over her as she tried again.

"Da... da... daddy?"

Tears welled up in Larry's eyes as he took Ash's hand.

"I'm here for you, baby," he said. "I'll always be here for you."

Ashleigh smiled, closed her eyes and dropped off to sleep.

As the weeks went by, Moru was becoming more and more concerned. Ash was struggling to walk and her speech was still slurred and hesitant. Moru's concern rested with the fact that she didn't seem to recognize him yet. The doctor had told him not to worry, because she couldn't remember the incident, either. When they asked her why she was there, she answered with a question: "Car accident?"

Once at home, Ash became a couch potato, sitting all day watching television. She left the house only to go to therapy. Penny noticed that whenever they drove past the park, Ash's expression became somber as she glanced toward the bench where the attack had occurred. It was obvious to Penny that she did not yet remember what had happened, but felt a strong familiarity with the site.

There was little solace in the fact that the police had identified Ash's assailants. They could not be located. There was hope that soon, someone would come forth to tell where the suspects were. Larry and Penny spent a great deal of time catering to Ash's every need while she was recovering. After weeks of therapy, she was able to take care of herself and her speech was slow and remained hesitant. She had difficulty concentrating and her schoolwork was mediocre at best, much unlike her past academic standing.

She had come to accept the fact that Moru was her brother, but could not understand how his eyes could be so different from hers. She had no recollection at all about what they had meant to each other and Moru was beginning to wonder if she ever would.

The months rolled by and it seemed that Ash had reached a plateau in her rehabilitation. Moru had gone off to college, crushed with the knowledge that his own true love didn't even remember him as her devoted lover. Like Larry, he often wondered if he was being punished for that past behavior.

It was almost a year since the attack. Moru was at college and Penny and Larry sat alone watching television. Ashleigh had gone to bed earlier because of a headache. Suddenly, they heard terrible screaming coming from Ash's room. They rushed up the stairs and opened her door to find her on her knees in the corner of the room, clutching her pillow to her body. Tears were streaming down her cheeks as she stared at them, wide-eyed.

"Don't let them touch me again!" she screamed.

Larry rushed to her, pulled her to her feet, and held her tightly.

"It's OK, honey," he spoke softly. "They're gone now. They can't hurt you any more."

"What happened to me?" she shouted hesitantly.

Penny approached and began rubbing Ash's back. "We'll tell you everything, sweetheart. Just calm down and know that you're safe now. What happened was a long time ago."

There was no further talking that night. Ashley's crying and trembling continued until she fell asleep and Penny laid her down and covered her. They both kissed her on the forehead and left her room.

"God, that was scary," Larry said. "I guess she's finally remembered."

Larry and Penny arranged to stay at home the following day in order to be there for Ashleigh. Her sudden recollection of the incident would likely prompt the flow of memories they were so eager to see return. Penny had reservations about having Ash remember her sexual relationship with her brother, but that was part of her suppressed memories, so they were bound to come to the fore eventually. They thought it fortunate that Moru was away, so that Ash would be able to deal with the flood of new information without his influence. Deep down, Larry hoped that the relationship between Ash and Moru would stay suppressed somewhere deep in her brain for a long, long time.

As they made their way downstairs in the morning, they checked on Ash, only to find she was not in her bed. Alarmed, they looked at each other and rushed downstairs, hoping to find her there. Ash was sitting back against the arm on the couch, her legs pulled up tight against her chest, her arms firmly clasped around them. Her eyes were wide, tears had stained her cheeks. She was looking nowhere in particular, seeing nothing.

"Ash, honey," Larry began, "are you OK?"

"Not really," she said softly. "I remember that two guys beat the hell out of me, but I don't know why." Her difficulty with speech was still evident, as she had to pause often to find the right word and enunciate it properly.

She shifted her position and lowered her feet to the floor. She fingered the scar that was still visible above her left eye where the plastic surgeon had closed a gaping gash.

"I get it now. I've been wondering what all the therapy was about and why I needed so many little surgeries. Just how much damage did those bastards do?"

They spent a long time explaining the extent of her injuries. Ash gasped when Penny mentioned the removal of her uterus and that it would mean no children. They cited the good luck with adoption they had had with Moru, but Ash didn't seem to care. As they sipped coffee, Ash started a series of questions.

"Was Moru there? At the park?"

"Yes, he was," Larry replied. "He was also badly beaten. He was attacked from behind, so he never saw what was coming."

"Did we go there often?"

"You two went everywhere together," Penny said reluctantly.

"Funny. I don't remember anything about Moru. Except, I know I knew him, but not how or why. Isn't that odd?"

"Don't worry about that," Penny said. "If you're meant to remember, you will, in time. There's a lot more healing to take place; more therapy; and I'm sorry to say, you have a few more surgeries until your face is back to normal. Then you'll have to be fitted with a partial plate to replace those broken teeth."

"Sounds like they're gonna erect a building."

"Rebuilding is a more appropriate term," Larry said with a slight smile.

"And don't be offended, but the doctor said when your memory comes back, you should see a psychiatrist."

"A shrink? Really? Wow. Just like a movie star."

Larry felt a sense of pride as Ashleigh showed some signs of her old spunk. He felt assured that the true healing was about to begin and that everything would soon be normal, not necessarily as it used to be, just normal.

Chapter 17

The surgeries ended over two years later. Ash looked pretty much as she did before the assault. Her speech patterns continued to reflect the problem that still existed in some parts of her brain. Her memory of Moru was still sketchy at best, and his absence didn't do much to reverse the process.

Moru had adjusted to his loss and was dating a girl at school. They had become quite fond of each other, but Moru couldn't think of a prolonged entanglement, in case Ash's memory came back. He was unsure of what he would do when that day came . . . *if* that day came.

When he and his girl friend Maris "discovered" each other sexually, the experience wasn't all Moru had expected. During the love making, he wanted the feel, the essence of the Ashleigh he had so deeply loved, but none of that was there. It was just plain sex; nothing like the thorough pleasures he once found with Ash.

Ashleigh, meanwhile, had lost all interest in sex and had no male friends to speak of. She went to her senior prom, but did no other socializing. She didn't want to go on with her education because of her speech difficulties. Instead, she poured herself into the study of piano and soon became quite proficient at reading and interpreting music, translating it into the language of the keyboard. Larry and Penny found a nice, upright piano for her and Ash treated it with loving care.

A quite evening at the St. Jacques' household was filled with soft piano music, muted television and an atmosphere of love. Often, Larry would stand behind Ash as she played, his hands resting lightly on her shoulders.

"You're good enough to play in public, Ash," he said to her one evening.

"Why would I want to do that?" she asked in her hesitant speech pattern.

"Because you love it so. You could bring all sorts of emotions to the surface for those who would hear you. You give me goose bumps and I'm sure you could do that for others, too."

"Oh, great," she said with a smile. "I could become Ashleigh Goosebumps!"

"Seriously, honey," Penny said, "that nice restaurant we love so much used to have a piano bar and now the piano just sits there all covered up. Maybe you could try playing some dinner music."

"Ah! So you two have been pl... pl... plotting. Why is it so hard to say that word?

"What do you say?" Larry asked. "Let's check it out."

Ashleigh could see the eager anticipation in their eyes. She grinned.

"What if I embarrass you?"

"You could never embarrass us, Ash. You're too good for that." Larry said.

Ash shrugged. "We'll see."

For two weeks, Ash worked hard on putting together two series of songs suitable for dinner background music. Something she had done since first starting to study piano was to hum and vocalize without words the tunes she was playing. She did this as she rehearsed and soon, Larry and Penny became enthralled with her performances.

The owners of the restaurant were friends to Larry and Penny and they knew Ashleigh's story. An arrangement was made that Ash could play during dinner three nights a week. At first, unknown to Ash, Larry would provide the funds to pay her, until the owners could see a link between business improvement and Ashleigh's appearances.

That came quickly. A microphone was placed atop the piano and wasn't even noticed by Ash as she sat down to begin her debut performance. Soft piano sounds filled the dining room at a volume that was comfortable enough to hear, but not intrusive on people's conversations. She began her singing that was not singing and the dining room became hushed. Her voice made lovely, haunting sounds that captured the attention of the diners. Even the servers made special efforts to make a minimum of noise so that each sound could be heard.

In her fourth week at the restaurant, Ashleigh's reputation had spread through town. The local newspaper interviewed her; radio talk show hosts featured her as a guest. On the radio, Ash said little, but played and hummed her way into the hearts of all who heard her. All the attention did wonders for her feeling of normalcy. She became more outgoing. It wasn't long before the restaurant owner's son, Dan, took an interest in her and soon after, they began dating.

Larry and Penny were ecstatic that Moru now had a girl and that Ash now had a boy. The stigma of their earlier incestuous relationship was now something locked away in a painful past.

"Have you ever wondered," Larry asked, "how we would have handled the sexual relationship between them if the assault hadn't happened?"

"All the time," Penny answered. "I've even felt guilty because I sometimes thought that the assault was a good thing."

"Me, too," Larry said. "As bad as it was, look at all the family turmoil we dodged."

It wasn't long before several local musicians who wanted to incorporate her "sound" into their own repertoires approached Ash. She declined them all and continued playing her dinner music at the restaurant.

Dan had always had an interest in jazz and exposed Ash to the music of some jazz greats like Stan Kenton, Dave Brubeck and Duke Ellington. Soon, Ash had adapted some of the jazzy highlights of the latest hits into her own inimitable styling.

Dan had a friend who worked at a production studio and he suggested that Ash produce a tape of her music. She agreed, thinking it was just a fling to satisfy her Dan, but her tape recording came out and was a hit on all the Boston area radio stations. It remained a regional hit for many months and her royalties, although not impressive, were a welcome source of income.

As the restaurant was closing one night, some of the old Ashleigh spunk surfaced. She made a bold sexual advance to Dan, paused, and then asked, "Do you want sex now or after we're married?"

Stunned, Dan looked at her and profoundly said, "Huh?"

"I just asked you to marry me, you jerk," she said smiling.

"But I wanted to do that."

"What, marry yourself?"

"No. I wanted to propose. Been thinking about for weeks."

"Then why didn't you ask? Is it my faulty speech pattern?"

"No. That's probably gonna get better in time, according to your dad."

"He's an optimist. But I do have to tell you something before we go any further. During the attack, I was sexually assaulted, too. I won't ever be able to have kids."

Dan said nothing. He studied Ash's face. Her expression didn't telegraph any message. Only a fixed stare, challenging him to respond.

"You mean you can't get pregnant?"

"That's usually what one does to have kids."

"Look, I love you. I want to marry you. If we want kids later, we can adopt like your folks did with Moru."

Ash wrapped him in her arms. They kissed passionately. Dan reached down and pulled her body tight to his.

"You kids gonna get married?" Dan's father spoke from the darkened back of the dining room.

They quickly separated and tried to look composed.

"Have you been listening?" Dan asked.

"No. I just came out of the kitchen and saw you two lip-locked. Looks like there's been more than dating going on."

Ash broke into a nervous smile and in her stammering speech pattern she said, "I asked him to marry me! It's not his fault."

Dan's father responded with, "Did he say yes?"

"Not yet," Dan said. "That kiss was the first part of my answer, which is 'yes'."

"It's about damned time," his father muttered as he returned to the kitchen area.

"I'm so sorry," Ash said, "I thought he was gone."

"Me, too. Want your ring now?"

"What?"

"I told you I wanted to ask you. I bought the ring last week."

"Well put it on my finger, you jerk! Looks like we were both planning it, huh?"

Ash looked at the ring he placed on her finger and smiled.

"We have to find someplace to have sex," Ash said. "Your dad might walk in on that, too."

They heard the car start. Glancing out the window, they observed Dan's father driving away. They turned to each other released their pent up passions.

After the sex, Dan still held Ash tightly. "Man, that was something," he said. "I love you even more now, and I didn't think that was possible."

"You're gonna squeeze the breath out of me," Ash said.

"Sorry." He eased his embrace and continued, "Was it good for you, too?"

"Oh yes," Ash lied. Actually, she had found it quite uncomfortable, but it was her first sex since the assault and she hoped it would get better in time.

Ash began to wonder why she had urges that called for sexual activity when the act itself was less than satisfying. Somewhere, sometime, she hoped to discover what it was she longed for in a sexual relationship. She and Dan would have to explore that together and she was certain that they could work out just about any problem that came along.

On the day of the wedding, Ash was tense, but not overly concerned with her relationship with Dan. It was comfortable. Perhaps that was all one could hope for. Comfortable.

Dan had no clue as to Ashleigh's problem. He was very much in love and enjoyed every moment, every touch, and every emotion that was endowed to him by Ash. Ash felt love for Dan, but the truly emotional exchanges left her wishing for more. Often, after a night of lovemaking, Ash would leave his bed and go to her piano. She would play softly late into the night. Dan would listen, smiling, until he drifted off to sleep.

Moru and Maris were in the wedding party. They openly expressed how happy they were for Ashleigh. Moru, however, could not help the feeling of loss that arose in his heart. When he took Ash into his arms to congratulate her, he nearly broke down and sobbed. He held himself in check, realizing that this would make for an awkward moment.

Ash and Dan were both beaming. It was their wedding day and they were happy. They were surrounded by friends and family and the love in the air warmed their many hearts.

At the reception that followed, Moru danced with Ashleigh.

"When are you and Maris getting married?" Ash asked him.

"What?"

"You heard me. You two have been going together long enough to have at least talked about it."

"Well, we haven't talked about it."

"What are you waiting for?" Ash asked. "You're both out of college now and have good jobs. Financially, it should be no problem. You having sex OK?"

"Ash! For Pete's sake!"

"Well, I know how it worked out with Dan and me. I would hope it would be as good for you, too."

"You are impossible," Moru muttered.

"That's no answer."

"And you're not getting one."

"What's the matter with you? I ask simple sister to brother questions and you get all hyper. Hell, look at you. You're blushing!"

"Quit it! And keep your voice down."

Ashleigh giggled and kissed him on the cheek just as Dan came up to them and cut in.

A relieved Moru rejoined Maris.

"You OK, honey?" she asked. "You look all flushed."

Moru smiled. "Just a little embarrassed," he said.

"What happened?"

"My sister asked me when you and I are getting married."

"Oh," Maris said after a pause. "What did you say?"

"Soon. As soon as you say 'yes'."

Maris smiled calmly. "Of course," she said.

"Should we make an announcement here?"

"Oh, my God!" Maris exclaimed. "You're serious!"

"I am. Are You?"

"Oh, yes! Announce away!"

Moru approached Ash after the meal had been served and asked her to announce his engagement before she left with Dan for their honeymoon. She leaped out of her chair and hugged her brother.

She stood at the microphone and commanded the attention of everyone in the room.

"Before Dan and I leave, I have an announcement," she said. Then she giggled. "I can't believe that a brother and sister can both be so happy on the same day. My brother, Moru, has proposed to his wonderful Maris, and she said 'yes'! Can you believe it? It must be this room so filled with joy and love that prompted that. A toast, everyone. To Moru and Maris!" She lofted her wine glass and said, "Long life and much love."

Penny squeezed Larry's hand tightly. *It's over for sure now. Their childhood "sexcapades" are well behind them now.*

"We dodged a bullet," Larry said quietly.

"Thank God. I've been worried about her remembering everything some day."

"That could still happen," Larry said.

"Yes, but they'll already be happily married by then."

"I hope so. All I hope for is that they'll be happy."

"Me, too," Penny said.

Chapter 18

Moru and Maris opted for a smaller, private wedding with few friends and family. It took place at a small country chapel near Beverly and the reception was more of a beach party than the more formal setting enjoyed by Ash and Dan.

It was a warm and sunny day and all the partygoers were dressed in their bathing suits and enjoying themselves. When Moru looked at Ashleigh in her Bikini swimsuit, he felt a return of those old emotions that used to inflame his desire in their youths. He had to force himself to take his eyes off her. He found that Maris was a tremendous help in this regard. She snuggled, nuzzled and kissed him often, diverting his attention to her. He felt a sense of guilt, feeling desire for his married sister, but what they had meant to each other years before could not be easily forgotten. Ashleigh still had no remembrance of their relationship, so from that standpoint, Moru felt a bit lucky. Had she felt the same desire, they would be right back where they were, probably alienated from their parents and likely scorned by their friends.

The long afternoon faded into dusk and the party broke up. The bond between Moru and Maris was now complete . . . a *fait accompli*. It served to ignite a new sense of passion in Moru that would be beneficial to Maris and to the solidity of their marriage. For some unknown reason to Moru, he underwent a catharsis and the desire for his sister, yielded to a desire for his new bride. He accepted his loss and turned all his energies into a focus on making his marriage work.

Work it did. Moru had his degree in finance and Maris soon became a certified public accountant. Moru worked at a financial planning firm, but Maris worked as a bookkeeper at home, because in less than a year, she was pregnant with their first child. Moru had come to realize a good measure of happiness from their union and was looking forward to the birth.

The entire family was excited about it, too. Ashleigh couldn't wait to be an aunt; Larry and Penny were excited about becoming grandparents ("young ones," Larry always inserted). Moru was sure it would be a son, but Maris didn't seem to care, as long as the baby had all its fingers, toes, and good health.

Larry remembered the joys of raising a young Moru and hoped for a boy. Penny was more hopeful for a girl. She had, as she put it, "already done that thing." She had urged Maris to have a sonogram to see the sex, but Moru and Maris preferred to wait until the birth to find out.

When that time came, Moru was out of town on business and Larry and Penny were not at home. Maris' water had broken and she needed to get to the hospital. Fortunately, Ashleigh was at home and hurried over, and bundled Maris off to the hospital.

The labor was brief and the birth occurred with no family present other than Ashleigh. That was enough. Both Maris and Ash were ecstatic. The baby girl was beautiful. Ash could hardly contain her excitement as she phoned Moru to give him the good news. She found Larry and Penny at home, just after they returned from shopping. In little over an hour, all the family members were there but Moru, who was now on his way home.

"You guys had a dozen names you were thinking on," Ash said. "What are you going to name her?"

"I want to wait for Moru," Maris answered.

"You mean you haven't decided?" Larry asked.

"We were close," Maris said. "We went through so many names it got downright confusing. We settled for a boy, but had a couple or so for a girl."

"When Moru gets here, we can all vote on it," Ash said excitedly.

Maris just smiled, then said, "I think we'll do it the traditional way. Moru and I will decide and probably disappoint everyone except us."

"Don't you worry about that," Penny said. "We'll love her no matter what you name her, but I hope it's a name that has grace and style."

"For Pete's sake," Dan said, "she's just a baby who's going to fill diapers and spit up on our best clothes. No name will offset that with style or grace."

"You are such a cynic," Ashley said, smiling. "Just be thankful that it won't be you changing the diapers and cleaning her little bottom."

"Oh, I am, I assure you."

"One of the names I liked was Melanie," Maris said.

"Oh, no. That's a lovely name but you can't pick a name we all like now, can you? I certainly like Melanie, too. Don't all of you think it's pretty?"

They all agreed, but Maris insisted that they had to wait for Moru. He arrived over an hour later and heartily approved of the name Melanie. Jokingly, he said he had hoped Maris would like Hildegarde, like the old singer. The moans and groans at the sound of *Hildegarde Saint Jacques* quickly changed to laughter when Moru winked at his sister.

Melanie St. Jacques captured the hearts of all the hospital workers in the maternity ward. Test after test only served to confirm her perfect state of health. In a matter of days, Maris and Melanie were back at home with grandparents and an eager aunt hovering about, in and out, and day after day. Maris was deliriously happy and wallowed in the warmth and love that surrounded them. *What a stroke of luck to have fallen into love with such a loving family!*

Moru had not only resigned himself to this marriage, with the arrival of Melanie his sense of devotion to this small family consumed him. He became an even more loving husband and father and although he still felt some remorse over the loss of his relationship with Ashleigh, it did not interfere with his responsibilities as head of a family.

Larry and Penny had settled into the roles of doting grandparents and as a couple, blessed the day that Moru and Ash had gone their separate ways.

Dan and Ashleigh, meanwhile, were having heated discussions about Dan's desire to own a motorcycle. Sometimes there was a bit of humor in their exchanges, but it was obvious that Ash was not in favor of such an idea. Dan brought Ash along with him to look at some motorcycles after pleading with her to just come with him and try riding with him. She acquiesced and soon found herself sitting behind Dan, her arms wrapped around him as the sped away from the dealership on a late model Harley Davidson. The ride was exciting and exhilarating. Dan got his motorcycle. They enjoyed long weekend rides together, but the motorcycle would prove to be a tragic mistake.

Not long after Dan made his purchase, he was sideswiped by a car and forced off the road. He and his motorcycle crashed into a tree and Dan was pronounced dead at the scene. It was more than Ashleigh could take. She suffered a complete breakdown.

The family, deeply mourning their loss, rallied around Ash to help her through the crisis. Nothing seemed to help. After days and nights of screaming and ranting in grief, Ash woke one morning and was suddenly calm and silent. Too silent. She spoke to no one. She responded to others but avoided having to express herself verbally. She avoided her piano; there was no music in Ashleigh's life anymore. The only sound was an occasional obscenity hurled into the silence around her. After several weeks, Larry took her to see the psychiatrist who had helped her through her earlier troubled state of mind.

She acknowledged his presence, nothing more. After three non-communicative visits, Larry and the doctor agreed that she should be hospitalized for aggressive treatments. The doctor explained that she could probably withstand shock treatments, even in light of her brain damage years earlier.

They admitted her to a hospital in Danvers, not far away. Larry and Penny visited several times a week. Dan's father visited on weekends. His mother talked with Ashleigh even though there was no response. Dan's father had nearly cried when he was told that Ashleigh was borderline catatonic.

Recovery was a long time in coming. Moru, Maris and Melanie visited often also, but their visits had little affect on her disposition. When she made eye contact with anyone, it made them very uncomfortable because of the hollow, empty look in her eyes. They were lifeless, without light, seemingly unable to decipher the visual messages received.

These discouraging visits went on for nearly a year until the first breakthrough occurred. Larry and Penny were visiting, talking to Ash, filling her in on what was going on in the family and the larger world around them.

Without any overture, Ash suddenly looked directly at Penny and asked, "Where's my brother?"

A stunned silence followed.

"I said, where's my brother?"

Penny stammered through her answer; "He'll come this weekend."

"Tell him to bring little Melanie. I haven't seen her in a long time."

Larry wanted to tell her that Moru and his family had visited every weekend all the time she had been here, but was afraid she might not understand.

"Good. I think I'm ready to go home now. Did I dream it, or is Dan dead?"

Penny looked at Larry, not knowing what to say.

Gently, Larry approached her and put his hand on her shoulder. "Yes, dear. That's why you're here. You completely broke down."

"I thought there was something like that. I had a lot of dreams. How long have I been here?"

"Almost a year," Penny said.

"Wow. When can I see my doctor?"

"We'll be sure he's contacted right away," Larry said.

"Good. How's the food here?"

"We don't eat here, honey, but you know, it's hospital food," Penny said. She couldn't believe that this conversation was taking place after the long months of silence.

Ashleigh had received several shock treatments during her stay, and Larry and Penny both felt that they must have triggered this sudden reversal in her condition.

Everyone was elated over Ash's recovery. In a matter of weeks, she had returned home and was acting more normal. When she entered her parents' house, she walked over to the piano and touched it fondly.

"I'll call the tuner tomorrow and have it fixed up for you," Penny said.

"That would be nice," Ashleigh replied. Then she turned, smiled, excused herself and went to her old bedroom. In the hallway, she paused at her door, turned and looked at Moru's door. She felt tingling warmth. She realized that she had a life to rebuild. It seemed this was not something new to her.

After the piano tuner left, she sat at the piano and looked at the keyboard for a long time. There was a piece of music on the stand and she picked it up. *Artistry in Rhythm,* a Stan Kenton standard. The melody came back to her and she started humming. Then she rested her hands on the keyboard and soon she was playing softly. Larry and Penny said nothing. They merely stood, watching, as tears ran down their cheeks. They had their little girl back.

There were more such moments over the weeks that followed. More and more, the old Ashleigh revealed herself. She played the piano every day and Dan's dad begged her to come back to the restaurant to play. It didn't take long before she decided to do just that and it was a bright moment for the entire family. Dan's father advertised that *Ashleigh was back!* And the restaurant's patrons responded. They kept the restaurant filled over that first weekend and Ash's spirits lifted. Indeed, she was back. She felt like she belonged again. Although she still mourned her loss, she now realized that she had a life to live and that it was time she moved on.

Moru, Maris and Melanie were real bright spots in Ash's life. She doted on her niece and felt strongly that this was her family now. Of course, that included Larry and Penny, but the *3M Company,* as she referred to Moru, Maris and Melanie, was now the center of the family circle. This was sometimes difficult for Moru who couldn't forget the passion that had existed between him and Ash when they were younger. He was truly in love with Maris and Melanie, but he was still excited around Ashleigh. He was able to suppress it but never dismiss it. Every time they were alone together, he so wanted to tell her, to see if he could jar those memories loose and bring them to the surface of whatever part of the brain was preventing it. *What the hell could you do about it if that happened? Nothing, that's what. Shit!*

Moru struggled with his dilemma for months, before he finally found a level of comfort. He was so aware that Ashleigh felt nothing like he did about their past that it became easier and easier to see it for what it was; just a series of misfortunes that he must deal with.

Ashleigh's speech continued to improve and she stammered only slightly now. She was a part of the furniture in the restaurant. On nights when she wasn't there, they needed only two waitresses. When she was there, they needed seven.

Life for the family had settled into a comfortable state of happiness. Everything seemed to become routine. There were no hitches or glitches. Melanie was growing like the proverbial weed and all the family energies were directed to the enjoyment of each other.

Chapter 19

For the first time since the assault, Ashleigh's general state of health started improving. She was at 118 pounds ever since her first hospitalization. She was now at 134 pounds and Moru jokingly called her "chubby." She had started wearing loose-fitting, floor length garments and had headbands made to match. Her tastes in colors and patterns were impeccable and the result was that every time she made an entrance at the restaurant, the patrons greeted her with applause.

She didn't realize that Dan was her second love lost and she had adjusted to being alone. She had her own small apartment not far from the restaurant, which was now operated by a management company. Dan's father was a consultant and still oversaw the menu and helped to develop new recipes.

After another successful evening, he approached Ash and asked her if she would like to buy the restaurant. It was something she had never considered, but promised him she would. There was coldness to the approach of the management company that displeased him. He felt it was time to cede or at least split ownership with a partner and hire a manager of their own.

After discussing her options with the family, they all agreed that it could be a good thing for her and they were all willing to help in any way they could. As evidence, they quickly came forth with the money that they needed to buy a half interest. Ash was excited at the prospects and stopped in to see Dan's father the next day.

"Marty, if you're serious about a partnership, my answer is 'yes', but I can't afford to buy it out. You're gonna have to stay on as my partner."

Marty smiled. "Dan would be so happy if he could hear this. It was going to be his restaurant, you know."

"Yes, I know, Ash answered. "When he bought that damned motorcycle he told me it would just be until he took over totally."

Marty nodded. "I'll make all the arrangements," he said. "Now I can feel happier about this. The restaurant will stay with family."

Once settled, Marty and Ash announced to their patrons what the new business arrangement was and they applauded and congratulated them. Marty, a widower for over eight years took a new interest in life. Ash's presence rejuvenated him. He started dressing "snappier" and paid more attention to his appearance. Once just a jeans and apron proprietor, he was now an elegant host who greeted his patrons, recommended wine choices and table-hopped like a professional.

One evening, a large party was celebrating an anniversary and feelings were high. Marty moved to the piano, and when Ash started playing and humming, he began singing the lyrics. The diners hushed and listened. This unlikely duo of a 60-year old man and this young thirtyish young lady made some beautiful music. The sound was unique and word quickly spread around town. Before long, on the nights when Ash and Marty performed, reservations were required well in advance. Business was good and Ash had to admit this was the happiest she had been since Dan's death.

Marty approached Ash after closing one evening.

"We make a good couple, you and me," he said.

"A better partnership I couldn't hope for."

"That's not what I mean. I mean the music we make."

"Yeah. It is pretty good, isn't it?" Ash said with a smile. "It's that rich, mellow sound of your mature voice that compliments my humming and vocalizing."

"No, it's your sound that does it. I mean you make the music follow and fit everything you do. And when I hold to the melody and lyrics, the sound is magic."

"I don't know about magic. I've heard that it's overrated, but I think there's been more of it in my life that I never got back when my memory returned. Somehow, I feel I've been cheated out of something."

"I'm sorry, but I think you have the magic, and you make the magic for others. You're a gift to everyone who knows you."

"Oh, my goodness! You sure have a distorted view of me."

"No, I don't. I want to make you as happy as you make others. I know I'm old enough to be your father, but I swear, I've fallen in love with you."

Ash was stunned. She looked at Marty and didn't see the 60-year old in front of her. He looked more like the young man Dan was the night he proposed. She remained silent.

"I'm sorry," Marty said. "I guess I'm just an old fool with a young man's mind."

"Well, don't beat yourself up. I'm flattered. But it's late. We'll talk tomorrow."

She left and neither said another word. Marty felt his heart pounding in his chest. *What a jackass. How could I even think she would care for an old fart like me?*

Ash went quickly to her car and started home. *What a sweet man. But he's so old. How could we possibly be compatible? We make sweet music together, but can we get beyond that?*

Both Marty and Ash suffered a restless night. They arrived at the restaurant before noon the next morning. The manager was already there and the place was set up for lunch. Ashley didn't usually come to the restaurant until an hour or two before the dinner crowd started arriving.

Marty came up to her looking apprehensive.

"Stopping in for lunch?" he asked. Then, "I'm sorry about last night. I don't know what I was thinking."

"Well, I will have lunch because I'm here, but I want you to join me."

Marty looked at her, not knowing what to expect. He said nothing, but joined her at the table when she sat.

"So, what do you have to say for yourself?" Ash asked.

"I'm not sure what you want me to say."

"Just what the hell were you asking me last night?"

"I don't think I asked anything. I just said I love you and if that offends you, I'm sorry and you won't ever hear me say it again."

Marty spoke so quickly that he was nearly breathless.

"But you were leading up to ask me something, weren't you?"

"Again, I'm not sure what you want me to say."

"Look, I'm your daughter-in-law and I fully expect you to love me. But, did you mean you loved me some other way?"

"Damn! I shoulda kept my mouth shut."

"That's not an answer."

Marty started to fidget nervously with his silverware.

"Well?" Ash asked.

"Well what? Do you want me to make a complete fool of myself? I know you can't feel about me like I feel about you and I don't know what made me think I could even approach the subject with you."

Marty spoke rapidly and he felt a pressure rising in his chest.

"But you did."

"Yes. And it has upset you and I'm so sorry," he said as he started to rise.

"Oh, sit down. I'm not upset. Just surprised."

Marty sat back in his chair again and asked, "What's that supposed to mean?"

"Just what I said," Ash responded, "I was surprised. I didn't think a mature man like you could see much in a half nuts middle-ager like me."

"I'm almost twice your age," Marty said.

"Who's counting?"

They became silent, just looking at each other. They ate lunch that way. No small talk, just silence. When they finished, Ash rose to leave.

"I'll be back for the dinner crowd. You better be in good voice tonight, because that's when you can start to woo me."

Marty was stunned. He never expected this! Ash didn't wait for any response. She whirled around and breezed out of the restaurant. Marty continue to sit there wondering what would happen next. *Could she actually care enough to become involved with me?*

The few hours before her return, time had seemed agonizingly slow. He was on edge and jittery. The manager asked if he was all right. Marty honestly didn't know.

During those same hours, Ashleigh was feeling a bit more positive than was Marty. She hadn't had any romantic interests since Dan's death and the fact that she felt so good about Dan's father bothered her just a little. *Would this be like incest?*

At that thought, Ash felt a strange stirring in her memory. She couldn't pull out anything that would support any memory involving a question of incest. She dismissed the thought, but wondered why it had evoked such a strange feeling.

That evening, Ash selected the songs they would do and they all had a touch of romance in them. For the first time since she started playing at the restaurant, she dared to sing the lyrics and was surprised that her stammering was not a problem. She vocalized cleanly and Marty was pleased with the result; so were the patrons.

When the evening ended and they were preparing to close, Ash approached Marty and put her arms around him.

"What if we're not sexually compatible?" she asked.

Marty didn't know what kind of an answer she expected.

"Well?"

"I hadn't given that a thought," Marty said.

"You men are all alike. You know damned well you've thought about bedding me, or it never would have come to your popping the question."

Marty blushed and said nothing.

"I didn't know guys your age could still blush," she teased. "You can kiss me if you want."

He wanted. He kissed her. It was warm, but little more than what Ash had experienced with her first tentative kiss with Moru. Like that first kiss, however, a flame was lit and soon they were pressed tightly together, kissing more intensely.

"I'm sorry," Marty said, "I didn't mean for anything more than that first kiss."

Ash smiled at him, saying, "Well, that first kiss wasn't enough. I wanted to see how much fuel you had left in your tank."

"What?"

"Let's just go to your office where we can take our clothes off and do this right."

"Are you sure you want to do this?" Marty asked, hoping for a positive response.

"I want to test the bicycle theory."

"The what theory?"

"You know," she said as they entered his private office, "once you learn to ride a bike you never forget." She began to disrobe. "So let's ride."

Neither of them had had any sexual activity for so long, the initial encounter was brief and less than deeply satisfying. After a while, the second attempt was considerably more comforting to each of them.

"Pretty nice, huh?" she asked.

"Nice? It was wonderful! I still feel odd about having sex with my daughter-in-law, though. Can't help but think it may not be moral, even if it is legal."

"Look, Dan's been gone a long time. Right now, we're just good friends, fellow entertainers; and I guess we're lovers now, too."

"Would you even consider marriage?"

"To whom?" she asked.

"I'm asking," Marty said. "Please don't make me grovel."

"If by grovel you mean more sex, then grovel."

Afterward, Ash took a deep breath and sighed it out.

She rolled over atop Marty and said with a smile, "Buy me a ring. If it wows me, I'll say yes, OK?"

"I'll get you a ring that'll knock your socks off."

He picked out a ring that had no central diamond. Rather, it was a small heart shaped ring of diamond chips, enclosing a brilliant ruby. When Ash saw it, she smiled at Marty and asked, "A church wedding or do we just elope?"

Chapter 20

Larry and Penny sat stunned. Ashley had just announced that she and Marty would be leaving for a week or two for the Bahamas, right after their wedding at city hall. Of course, the family was invited. She talked of the warm feelings she and Marty had for each other.

"He's old enough to be your father," Larry said after a pause.

"And it takes more than warm feelings to make a good marriage," Penny added.

"But he makes me happy. It's been a long time since I could say that. I'm happy."

"What happens if you are not compatible?" Penny asked.

"Oh, that's no problem. For the age difference, I'd say we're plenty compatible."

"You mean . . . oh," Larry said.

"You seem to have a penchant for testing the definition of incest, Ash. Good grief, he's your father-in-law," Penny said.

"It's funny you should use that word," Ash said. She felt that strange prodding at her memory she had the last time she had thought about it. "Father-in-law is a title that assumes the presence of a son and husband. Neither exists now. We're just lovers who are going to get married."

"How much time have you devoted to considering this?" Larry asked.

"Marty has been thinking about it longer than I have, and he's sincere. Look at this ring."

She held out her hand for them to see the ring Marty had given her.

"A nice ring doesn't prove anything," Penny said. Her mind was in a whirl. She recalled the hot, sexual relationship Ash and Moru had engaged in leading up to the assault that changed their lives. Ash's long recovery, prolonged periods of therapy; Moru's anguish over Ash's loss of memory of their sexual activity, now just a blank hole in her memory bank. *How much more turmoil could this girl bring into their lives?*

"Well, I'll let you know when we get hitched and you can come if you want to."

Larry stood and approached Ash. He put his arms around her. Ash didn't struggle, but stiffened.

"Relax, honey. Of course we'll come. All we've ever wanted is your happiness. You've been cheated out of it often enough. We're certainly not going to argue with you if you're sure it's what you want."

"I'm sure, daddy."

Penny looked at the two of them and softened.

"Don't let this old witch spoil anything for you, Ash. If you feel this is best, I'm all for it, too. Now get over here a hug the old lady."

Larry and Penny murmured their congratulations and Ashleigh left. She was elated at the way she had left it with her parents and virtually skipped to her car.

"You know," Penny said as she watched Ash drive away, "that girl has always had an 'on' switch in the 'off' position. First, it was Moru, then Dan, now Dan's *father!* What's wrong with her?"

Larry paused, then answered, "Maybe we should ask what's *right* with her."

"Right? What could be right? First, she seeks sex with her own brother; then she marries after an unbelievable traumatic event; now, she's having sex with her father-in-law! What could be right about that?"

"Well, we can't get inside her head. Maybe she sees nothing wrong. After all, she's looking for what's right and all we're looking at is what we consider wrong."

"Defend her if you want to, but I wonder if her mother had the same warped sense of values."

Larry said nothing.

"Oh, nuts. I didn't mean that."

Larry left the room. Penny stared after him. *Oh, my God. Is he still in love with her after all this time? Or is it just the memory he's in love with? Shit! My mouth overloaded my brain again!*

She followed Larry out of the room and found him in the kitchen fixing a cup of coffee. He seemed to be ignoring her.

"I'm sorry," she said, "that was uncalled for."

"Don't think I haven't wondered, too."

"It's just that since she came to us, it's been one bizarre event after another. It was sex with her brother, then we almost lost her. She came out of it less than whole, but she learned to play piano and make a go of it. Then there was Dan and that damned motorcycle. And just when we thought she was all right, she comes in and announces that she's marrying her father-in-law! And to top it all off, she's not the biological daughter we thought she was."

"Well," Larry replied, "you've just condensed her entire life into that short outburst. You failed to mention the good times. Our Sunday picnics when she was young. The trips to the shore where she played in the water with all of us. The delights of hearing her play the piano here and at the restaurant. Maybe she has her idiosyncrasies, but overall she's a delightful creature."

"She's a mystery to me. I love her; I truly do, but she can test that love and *has* tested it over and over. I hope I can stay strong enough to tolerate it."

"Tolerate what?"

"Her unpredictability. Every time she walks through that door, I wonder what's next."

"Well, it seems that future surprises will be reserved for Marty. Maybe we should hope that he's strong enough to tolerate her adventures."

The wedding occurred two weeks later in the presence of a Justice of the Peace. He at least had the semblance of an altar in a small foyer, candles and taped organ music. It wasn't the religious ceremony Larry and Penny had hoped for, but they managed to achieve a level of dignity that made the marriage seem more credible. "It beats City Hall," Larry thought.

"I'm exhausted," Ash said at the small reception at the restaurant.

"My first wedding wasn't near as tiring as this one. I must be getting old."

"I'm still OK," Marty said. "The old adrenaline is flowing, I guess."

"You're just getting horny," Ash smiled back at him.

"That, too," he replied.

"We don't have much time," Ash said as she looked at her watch. "Our flight leaves in just three hours."

"The car's loaded and ready to go. Let's circulate and start saying our goodbyes."

In less than ten minutes, they were on their way to the airport. There they boarded their flight to the Bahamas for a brief honeymoon. Marty jokingly called it a vacation, fearing he was too old to withstand the rigors of a real honeymoon.

Moru had finally accepted that there was no future for him now with Ashleigh. After all, they were middle-aged, had other interests, and in Moru's case, a family. He was devoted to Maris and Melanie and everyone in the extended family had reached a level of comfort with the way things were.

Marty and Ash were only gone for two weeks. When they returned, Ash was suffering from a severe case of the flu, which had spoiled the last three days of their honeymoon. They quickly settled into their routine; early dinner at the restaurant followed by playing and singing for their patrons. Soon, Marty was singing more solos, as Ash's voice weakened. The flu had held on for several weeks. She would have good days when she thought she had finally licked it, but it soon came back, each time seemingly stronger than the last. When she suddenly announced that she felt too tired to perform, Marty became concerned and they scheduled a doctor visit.

Four visits later, after a battery of lab tests, Marty and Ash sat in the doctor's office. Marty was stone-faced, Ash said nothing, but tears rolled down her cheeks.

"You have AML; myelogenous leukemia," the doctor had announced.

After a pause, he went on.

"There's a five year survival rate of forty percent with proper chemotherapy treatments."

"This is what killed my mother," Ash said looking at Marty.

"Yes," the doctor went on, "you have what we call a genetic disposition to the disease. We can start chemotherapy immediately and we should be able to give you a number of years in a remissive state."

"Bullshit," Ash said.

Both Marty and the doctor looked at her in surprise.

"Relax, honey," Marty said. "That's no way to respond."

"Listen, I lived through all this with my mother. There's no way I'm going to allow that. I'm not going bald; I'm not puking my guts out every day after treatments. I guess you can say that I've seen the future of this thing and I'm not playing the game."

"Are you refusing treatment?" the doctor asked.

"You bet I am. Just give me what I need to fight the infections when I get them and to ease the pain when I need it. Let this damned germ die with me."

Marty gave a short gasp. "You can't mean that."

Ash looked tenderly at Marty. "I'm so sorry," she said. "You don't deserve this. I just wish we had learned about it before we got married. Now you have to bear the same pain I did, watching my mother die. At least, I won't hang on so long and suffer the humiliation of chemotherapy."

"But, Ash honey, we have to fight this thing. We could have years more together."

"Sure. Years of agony. Me wasting away, going bald, getting emaciated. You can tell all our friends at the restaurant, 'Look at the skeleton at the piano! That's my wife! You remember Ashleigh, don't you?' Then they can look at me in disbelief."

"Stop that," Marty said, obviously hurt. "We can go home and discuss this."

"Nothing to discuss. I know what's coming and I'm not opting for the end like my mom had. I just want out. Out of a life that's been shitty for a long time. I'm not going to make it worse by undergoing a chemical crap shoot."

She walked to the door with a confident stride. She looked back at Marty who was too stunned to move.

"Oh, come on, Marty. You know I didn't mean you were part of that. Let's go. We have a lot of living to do in a short time. Let's not waste any of it."

"Please take my advice," the doctor said as they were leaving. "We've made great strides in chemotherapy over the past few years."

The door closed quietly behind them. The doctor looked at the door, then down at the records in his hand, and shook his head.

For over a month, Marty and Ashleigh made the best of their situation. Marty frequently had to make excuses for Ash's absence from the restaurant. He often lied to Larry and Penny, assuring them had Ash was just a little under the weather. He could no longer blame the flu that seemed to have been the trouble when they returned from the Bahamas.

Ashleigh slept well into mid-morning every day now. Marty spent much time with her, assuring that she ate, even though she had little desire to do so. The headaches had begun and were a daily occurrence. She grew pale and suffered from diarrhea and a general state of malaise. It wasn't long before they had to tell Larry and Penny, who were devastated by the news. A month later, Ash was bedridden and Marty had hired a night nurse to be with her while he was at the restaurant. Time was growing short and Larry knew that he had better prepare Moru for what was happening.

"Why didn't you tell me sooner?" Moru demanded.

"We haven't known that long," Larry told him. "When Marty told us, the disease had progressed so far that we were shocked when we first saw her."

"I have to see her," Moru said.

"Of course; call Marty and find out when's the best time."

"Oh, God," Moru said trying to fight off the tears. "I've never stopped loving her, but I knew it was no good."

"And now you have Maris and Melanie to think about."

"Don't you think I know that? Hell, I watched her come out of that beating not remembering me. I saw her marry Dan, then along came Marty. It seems everyone got to share her love but me and I'm the one who truly loved and wanted her. Sometimes I've felt that I was trapped in a marriage of convenience."

"You don't mean that. You've had a solid marriage."

"Because we worked at it. Maris didn't know about Ash and me, but she knew that something was eating at me."

"Well, you have to find a way to put it behind you. You know the old cliché, life goes on."

"Crap!"

"Yeah, I know. Your mom and I, well, we were shocked about you two when we found out. I'm not sure what might have happened if you hadn't been attacked that night. Penny was truly hurt; I was just flabbergasted."

"We probably would have run away as soon as we were old enough to get away with it. If we couldn't get married, we would have just lived together. Dammit, dad, we *really loved each other.*"

"We thought it was just raging hormones, you know. Teenagers are like that. But, by blood or on paper, you *were* brother and sister!" Larry said emphatically.

"Not much to argue about now, is there? I still don't think it was that wrong, but it is part of the past that will be soon forgotten by everyone but me."

"I don't think you should necessarily forget it. I doubt that you could. But a chapter is closing here. You can grieve for your sister, but you can't grieve what could never have been."

"It's a first love lost," Moru said. "You can identify with that. Ash told me all about you and her mom. That was a first love lost, too. Don't you still grieve over that?"

Larry didn't answer.

"Well, do you or not?"

"That's a pretty blunt way to put it," Larry said. "I'm not sure *grieve* is the right word. I do regret the unfortunate circumstances that ended it for us. But I got a second chance; a chance to renew the magic. It wasn't there. Things change. Had Ash's memory of your relationship. . ."

"It was love, not a relationship," Moru interrupted.

"If her memory returned after the incident, how do you know the magic would still be there? You were both thoroughly traumatized. All you remember is what you focused on, and that was probably just the sex."

"If I could have reached her, if you had let me, I think she would have come out of it for me."

"I'm afraid we've exhausted this subject. We have to agree to disagree. Your sister is dying and no matter how we see the past, that fact is undeniable."

"I'm going to see Marty. We share a common grief."

"Don't do anything foolish."

"Don't worry. I couldn't do anything to hurt Marty or sis at a time like this."

"Well. You called her 'sis', son. Was it that hard?"

"I've called her that lots of times. But I know I called her Ash almost all the time. I usually said 'sis' when there were others around."

"Go see Marty. Try to be strong for each other."

Chapter 21

Moru and Marty met at the restaurant. When Moru entered, he noticed that Ash's piano was covered with flowers from patrons. He felt a shudder as he noted how like a funeral arrangement it appeared to be.

"How bad is she?" Moru asked.

Marty just shook his head. "I didn't think it could be this fast. It's how she wanted it. She said it wasn't fair that she be a burden for a couple of years like her mother was."

"I wish you could have told me sooner."

"Ash didn't want anyone to know until we couldn't hide it any more."

"How long since she played the piano here?"

"Almost a month. When your folks came in I told them she was just taking a night off. Fortunately, they didn't come in that often or they would have gotten wise."

Moru looked at Marty. He noticed that Marty had a tired, drawn look about him. His shoulders, usually back and squared, now had a slump to them, as in one recently defeated. There were dark circles under his eyes, and his usual smiling mouth was set in a grim line, with corners down-turned. Moru realized that Marty was already in mourning for Ash; *their* Ashleigh.

"Is there a best time for me to visit?" Moru asked.

"You're her brother, man. Visit when you like. I'm sure she'll love it."

"I meant, is there a best time for her?"

"Oh. Well, she sleeps most of the day. It's the painkillers. Usually, in the early evening, I sit on the edge of the bed and we have a cup of soup together. If you came around, say at eight o'clock, she should still be pretty lucid."

"Lucid? You mean she gets delirious?"

"Sometimes. I don't know why, but evening seems to be her best time. You should come then. During the day, she snores a lot."

"Why aren't you with her this evening?"

"Manager had a problem. I'm going home in about an hour. Why not come with me?"

"It's almost nine. Will she still be awake?"

"I think so. The evening cup of soup has become a ritual and if she's asleep, I'm supposed to wake her. So, come on along. Maybe you two can talk after the soup."

They left together. There was a chill in the air. Moru got into his car and followed Marty to his house.

Thanksgiving was only two weeks away, but neither Moru nor Marty felt there was much to be thankful for. They entered the living room, pausing before going to Ash's bedroom.

"I hope she can last until Thanksgiving," Marty said.

"Why?" Moru asked, "What's to be thankful for?"

"For the time we had with her. I know it wasn't very long for me, but it was quality time. I almost envy the fact that you had so much more time with her."

Moru felt an uncomfortable feeling in the pit of his stomach as he said, "Well, after all, she was my sister. We lived in the same house."

"Oh, I know," Marty said. "You two had that sibling love thing. The intimacy I knew with Ash was all too brief. I just want to hold her again. Oh, hell, I'm sorry. I know you don't think of your sister that way."

Moru said nothing, but inside his head, he could hear his voice screaming. *I loved her first! She was the love of my life!*

"Man, I don't know why I would say such a thing."

Moru calmed himself. "Don't worry about it."

Marty eased the door open and observed Ash, propped up on pillows. The night nurse arose from her chair at bedside. Looking at

Ashleigh she said, "There we are. I told you he would be here soon. And he's brought company."

Ash looked at Marty and smiled. She turned to look at Moru and a frown came across her face. Then, her eyes widened in recognition. "Moru! Moru! You came."

Moru forced a half smile as he reached for her hand. It was a cool, bony hand, skeletal in appearance. She looked so small and frail, Moru had to fight back the tears. Could this be his Ashleigh? Was this that sexy, energetic young girl who was his very first?

"Why didn't you let me know?" he asked. Tears filled his eyes and spilled out over the lids.

"Didn't want to be like my mother."

"What?"

"She took too long to die. It was rough. Didn't want to do that."

"Damn it, girl, we love you. We could have gotten through anything together."

"Not this. Oh, soup!" Her eyes lit up slightly as the night nurse entered the room with two cups of soup.

"Would you like some?" the nurse asked Moru.

"None for me, thanks."

Moru watched as Marty sat on the edge of the bed and helped Ashleigh set the cup of soup on her bedside tray. They spooned out a little and sipped. They looked fondly at each other. Moru could see the depth of their relationship and suddenly felt happy that they could enjoy each other at such a trying time.

"Seen mom and dad?" Ash asked of Moru.

"Last night. They're fine. Send their love."

She and Marty continued sipping their soup, saying nothing, but staring at each other throughout the time they spent eating their soup.

"How's it been this evening?" Marty asked as he handed the near empty cups back to the nurse.

"Tired. Hardly could stay awake for you. Headache's worse. Nurse says my fever's up again. Took aspirin."

Ash's speech pattern was jerky with each thought expressed as stand-alone statements. She still had occasional trouble putting a sentence together since the assault and thus spoke slowly and cryptically.

The nurse had left the room, so Moru took her chair and drew it more closely to Ash's side. Marty was on the edge of the bed near her knees. Moru reached out and took Ash's hand.

"Are you comfortable?" Marty asked her.

"Hell no," she said. "I'd like to get up for a while, but it makes me so damned tired."

"Here," Moru said, "sit in this chair for a while. Maybe it'll make you feel better."

"Fat chance," she said, but she sat up with a smirk and a half smile.

Marty and Moru helped her settle in the chair. Marty wrapped a blanket around her legs, leaned forward and kissed her on the forehead. She reached up, placed her hand on Marty's cheek, and smiled up at him.

Moru's heart felt like it was breaking. Although Ash was around the same age as he, Moru noted that her frail and withered condition made her look as old, even older than Marty. He stood behind Ash and placed his hands on her shoulders. Such bony shoulders, he thought.

There was no conversation now, as Ashleigh promptly nodded off to sleep.

"Boy," Moru said, "that was fast."

"Yeah. Just getting out of bed wipes her out. Let me get her back into bed."

As Marty was settling her in, she mumbled a little, gave a half smile and went out again.

"She'll be good for the night, now," Marty said. Tears were streaming down his cheeks.

Moru controlled himself no better. He sat back down and took Ash's hand.

"Mind if I stay with her for a while?" Moru asked.

"No. When you're ready, come out to the kitchen. I need a stiff drink."

"Yeah, I'll be along in a few minutes."

Marty went out to the kitchen and the night nurse retired to the guest bedroom for the evening. In the kitchen, Marty poured himself a stiff five ounces of Jack Daniels. Moru sat at Ashleigh's bedside and finally broke down. He lowered his head onto the bed and wept, mourning his loss.

As the evening wore on, Marty fell asleep at the table, his empty whiskey glass still in his hand. Moru fell asleep, cried to a point of exhaustion, his head on Ash's bed, her hand still in his.

It was after midnight when Moru stirred. Ashleigh was mumbling. Her eyes opened and she looked at Moru.

"Moru? Is it you?"

"Of course it's me. Are you OK?"

"Moru? Oh, my God! You're Moru. My Moru. My first love."

Moru was stunned! *She remembered! After all this time, she remembered that they were first lovers!*

"You remember!" he said in a forced whisper.

"Yeah."

"Welcome back," Moru said, thinking it a stupid thing to say.

"Did they get 'em?"

"Who?"

"The guys who did this to us."

"Yeah, but not for that. They robbed a bank and got caught."

"Good," she said. "Fry their asses."

She became quiet. Moru thought she had fallen asleep again.

Moru felt a feeble squeeze of his hand as she murmured, "We were pretty damned good together, huh?"

"We were something special," Moru answered.

Then she drifted off once again.

The time of death was officially listed around three A.M. Her husband was asleep at the kitchen table. The night nurse was asleep in the guest room. Her brother sat at her bedside, holding her hand as it grew colder in his. He was awake, staring as if in a trance.

He alerted Marty and the nurse when he composed himself, then went to the kitchen and with tear-filled eyes, poured himself a stiff drink of Jack Daniels.

It was a closed casket funeral, with burial on Thanksgiving Day. It was Marty's choice of day. He told everyone he wanted to bury Ashleigh on that day so that he could express his thanks for the short time they had together. It was hard on everyone and other than the funeral, there were no other activities on that day for the family.

Later, with Larry and Penny, Moru, Melanie and Maris were seated around the table having a modest meal. Afterward, Larry and Moru went out onto the back porch. Larry carried a bottle of whiskey and two glasses. Outside, Moru looked at Larry.

"What's with the booze?"

"Just think we should make a toast, son. Just you and me."

"To Ash?"

Larry poured whiskey into the two glasses and handed one to Moru.

"Actually, a toast to first loves lost; to my Ashley; to your Ashleigh; to you and to me."

They touched glasses and downed the whiskey.

end